CHARLIE'S GOLD

and other

FRONTIER TALES

BY
KENT KAMRON

CHARLIE'S GOLD
and other
FRONTIER TALES

PUBLISHER'S NOTE
This is a work of fiction. Names, characters, places and incidents either are the
product of the author's imagination or are used fictitiously, and any resemblance to
actual persons, living or dead, events, or locales is entirely coincidental.

Author - Kent Kamron
Publisher - McCleery & Sons Publishing
Editor in Chief - Steve Tweed

International Standard Book Number 0-9642510-9-4
Printed in the United States of America

FORWARD

The western tales crafted by Kent Kamron are satisfying, like a hot tin of beans under the chilly skies of high plains country. Not since the prolific Louis L'Amour has a writer of the pioneer fable so deftly captured the rough hewn sights and crackling sounds of the Old West. Readers may well be reminded of the best dialogue from classic Fifties television shows such as *Gunsmoke, Have Gun Will Travel* or *The Rebel*. The title story, "Charlie's Gold", invokes images of the desperate greed which foiled the characters in John Huston's famous film, *Treasure of the Sierra Madre*.

It's unusual to see such descriptive, fast-paced short stories these days, and I, for one, was pleasantly surprised to discover Kamron's work. I know the author, and can vouch for his personal history of wartime adventure and his multi-faceted interests. But I was unaware that Kamron had been hard at work recreating the Wild West until I read this collection. He has captured the gritty, masculine world of the gunslingers and prairie scavengers, but not at the expense of his able treatment of women's themes. And readers yearning for Native American characters who possess breadth, bravery and rich humor won't come away disappointed either.

To publish the first collector's series of Kent Kamron's stories is a pleasure indeed for McCleery and Sons. We trust that we will be bringing other works by the author before the public in ensuing months and years.

Steve Tweed
Editorial Director
McCleery and Sons Publishing

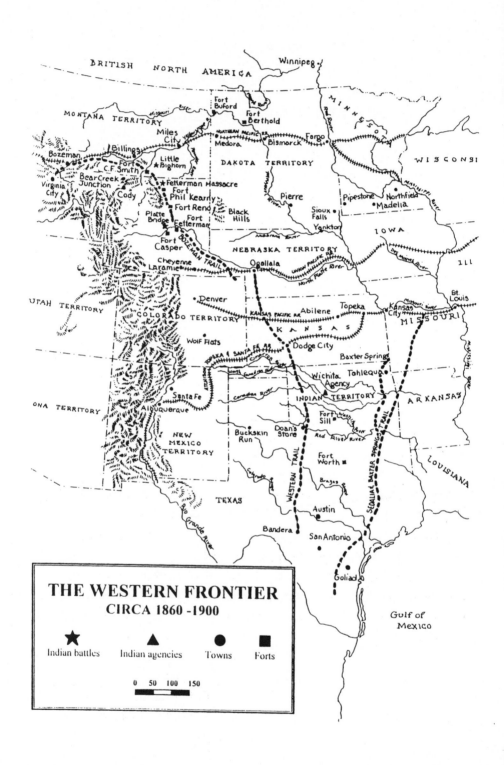

THE WESTERN FRONTIER
CIRCA 1860 -1900

★ Indian battles   ▲ Indian agencies   ● Towns   ■ Forts

0   50   100   150

TABLE OF CONTENTS

FROM THE AUTHOR

I wanted to be a cowboy ever since the first time I saw Roy Rogers on the silver screen. I dreamed about riding the rodeo circuit and owning a ranch, but in truth I never bought my first horse until I was 52 years old. I never owned a ranch either, although right now I have my eyes on a piece of land. I have, however, been thrown from a horse quite a few times, which sort of qualifies me for something.

The Dakotas have been my home all these years. I started out in a little town by the name of Tyndall, South Dakota, spent most of my early schooling in Sioux Falls and somehow ended up in Fargo, North Dakota. Not everybody thinks of the Dakotas as being the real west, but they were at one time. I happen to think they still are, but I might be a bit prejudice. However, if you ever visit us, you'll discover we have our share of wide-open ranch country. I love it when I can see fifty miles in every direction.

Reading western non-fiction is one of my favorite pastimes, and if I had to do it all over again, I think I would have been a teacher of cowboy history. But in retrospect, what we study for and what we end up doing—and what we think we should have been doing are often three different things.

This passion I have for writing seems to be unending. We all have a hundred stories inside us; it's just a matter of digging them out and getting them on paper. If you have read Louis L'Amour, one of the best western writers of our time, you'll know what I mean.

The setting for a lot of the stories in this collection is in places I've traveled to, which gives several of the tales some historical credence. A couple of them are based on real, historical characters and situations, and in a few I got a bit personal. For instance, you'll learn my horse's name in *The Hanging of Frank Behm,* and when you read *Man of Teeth,* you'll know just how I felt when I had to put my horse down a few months back. Now and then I've shaped characters in my tales after some of my friends. A handful of these stories first appeared or have been accepted for publication in some small literary magazines. My appreciation goes to *Words of Wisdom, Timber Creek Review, My Legacy* and *Western Digest.*

Putting these stories together was a family effort, so I have a lot of friends to thank for their participation. First thanks goes to my wife, Ver, for all those nights I deprived her of sleep, just so I could read a few pages of the day's efforts. Besides her, there's Marty and Sharon and Ted and Tony and Merry, all good readers with good suggestions. For all you others, who put in your two bits at one time or another, my hat's off to you, too.

My sincere thanks goes to Steve and McCleery & Sons Publishing Company for believing these stories had some merit. And a special thanks to Mark Vinz, one of the finest poets in the Upper Midwest, who got me started writing so many years ago.

***

Kent Kamron

Dedicated to my wife
and two sons

INCIDENT IN THE BIG HORNS

"You're crazy to go on alone." That's what Colonel Leavens, the Commander at Fort Phil Kearney told Roy Caldwell. If Roy would wait another week to ten days, a freighter would be coming through, at which time Colonel Leavens would provide an escort as far as Fort Smith, 75 miles ahead. But Roy Caldwell was his own man. He had wrangled in his earlier years, driven cattle from the Rio Grande to Denver, fought his way back through Indian country, and on more than one occasion had quit an outfit just because he didn't like the way the foreman chewed his morning bacon.

His brother and a job were waiting for him in Bozeman, and no army officer, colonel or not, was going to tell him what to do.

"I come all the way from Nebraska Territory," he told the Colonel. "And I don't think there's anybody big enough around here to stop me." That was powerful talk from a man who barely weighed 130 pounds. Roy Caldwell wore a Dragoon six-shooter on his hip. The Dragoon was a heavy pistol, and the weight alone left the tip of the barrel just a few inches above his knee.

Colonel Leavens knew he was up against an obstinate man. "If I was you, I'd ride a mile or two off the trail," the officer advised when he realized Roy was intent on continuing by himself. "The Sioux spend weeks on end waiting for a loner to come along. You'd be the easiest scalp they ever got." Roy had enough advice. He picked up some dried jerky and a few canned goods at the general store and headed out late in the afternoon.

Within a few miles of the Fort he passed the site where young Lieutenant Fetterman and some eighty of his men had been wiped out by the Sioux. That was just a few years back. Crazy Horse was responsible for that massacre, Roy Caldwell knew. Though he was not a good reader, he had managed to glean some information from a newspaper at the time, and had heard enough talk about the massacre to know when and where it took place.

Out of bitterness, Roy stuck to the trail. It wasn't any secret he was stubborn, and he knew it. Sometimes he was even mean, but only when meanness was called for. He had gained a name over the years for being potentially ornery, and he knew that, too. In fact he had once killed a man. The man had cheated him at cards, and when Roy had called him on it, the man drew a pistol. Roy was faster, even though he had pulled the big Dragoon, and he had purposely shot the man in the arm to keep from killing him. But the card cheater went about his way, and didn't bother to have the arm looked at by the town Doc. A week later gangrene placed him into an early grave. Now there was a man who was too stubborn, Roy Caldwell was thinking to himself as he urged his sorrel into a trot.

Yes, Roy was a lot of things, but he had never cheated a man in his life, and he couldn't stand to be around anybody, man or woman, who even hinted at being just a tinge crooked. Anybody that knew Roy Caldwell knew him to be a man of his word, and honest to boot. Those were probably two of his best qualities.

Towards evening Roy crossed a fork of the Tongue, located a hollow off the trail and bedded down for the night. By sunrise he was up, packed, and on his way. He had barely covered two miles when he came across a fresh trail. He could tell by the matted down grass, perhaps three or four horses had passed through here, and more than likely this morning. He could see where the fresh trail led over a rise a half mile ahead. He set his sorrel into a trot and pursued the tracks. At the top of the rise, he held up suddenly.

"Would you look at that, Coley?" he said to his horse. About a half-mile ahead three Indians were riding away from him in the direction of the Bozeman Trail. He was not worried, since he could see all three were carrying bows, with quivers visible strapped to their backs. Roy had a Henry rifle in the scabbard attached to his saddle. The Henry could drop each of them five times off their horses before they could get within a hundred yards of him. But that was not at all his intention.

He backtracked a bit, but kept a careful watch as he rode parallel to the three Indians. For most of the day, he trailed along in this fashion, keeping out of sight, amused that it was usually Indians who stalked a white man, not the other way around.

And he had been cautious. This was just a small party, perhaps hunters, or perhaps a party with intentions of finding a loner like himself on the trail. But for most of the day, they did not appear to be a threat, and it was obvious they did not expect somebody to be observing them from behind. Their gaze and attention seemed to be focused on the trail below.

That night Roy made a cold camp, considering it practical not to risk a fire and give away his position. In the morning, he headed out toward the north again in the same direction he had been moving all along.

Almost immediately he came across their trail. The three Indians had spent the night no more than three or four hundred yards from where he had camped! He didn't know if they had built a fire, since he had smelled no smoke, however, the wind had been coming down off the Big Horns, passing toward the east.

He spent half the day trailing them as he had the day before, and by early afternoon, he had enough of this cat and mouse game. The three were headed north, the same as he, and it was possible they were a scouting party from a larger band up ahead. Off to his left he could see a narrow pass that led through the Big Horns. He knew that at the top at this time of year in June, there would more than likely be snow, but that was not a deterrent.

"Come on, Coley," he said to his sorrel. "With a little luck we can make it over that pass before nightfall." Once on the other side, he could make for the Bighorn River, parallel that north and pick up the Bozeman Trail on the far side of Fort Smith.

He kept to the tree line as much as possible on the way up the mountain side, always looking back, keeping the three Indians in view. After a few hours, he was high enough that he had a command of the open plains to the east. The three Indians and their horses were like worms now, so distant they were. For them to catch a glimpse of him was near impossible.

He continued at an easy pace up the side, feeling the chill of the evening coming on. He loosed the straps behind his saddle and pulled at his coat. For the past hour or so, they had been walking in snow. Up ahead, the saddle ridge couldn't be more than an hour or so away. Roy studied the landscape and noticed off to his left what appeared to be a natural path. He headed his horse in that direction and followed the way, but as he moved upward the path began to narrow and after another few hundred yards, the path led around a rather steep incline. Yet the path looked solid, and when Roy urged his horse onward, it suddenly happened.

The rocks beneath Coley's feet loosed and he reared up. With the weight on his back legs, a shelf of snow gave way and Coley lost his footing. It happened so fast, Roy Caldwell barely had a chance to react. Knowing that Coley was going down, he leaped from the saddle and landed flat in the snow, face first, his hands jammed in as far as they could reach. As if holding on for dear life, he remained still and heard the threshing of Coley as he rolled down with the small avalanche of snow. Seconds later, Roy turned to see his horse below, safe, but standing in snow up to his chest and unable to fight his way back up the bank. Roy quickly assessed his own situation. If he moved, it was very possible the snow beneath him might slide, just like with Coley. He held his breath, unsure what to do. But there was no other choice. Coley was in a deep depression. If Roy slid down the embankment, he did not think he would be able to climb back out. And at the bottom, even though he would have access to his lariat, there was nothing above to toss his lariat around. No rocks, no stumps, nothing. He took a deep breath, then eased one hand upward and plunged his gloved hand into the snow, moving only inches at a time. His progress was slow but steady, and eventually he reached the path, sweating about his face. Surprisingly, his hat was still in place.

He stood now and looked below. Coley was at least thirty feet away and fighting to gain his footing, but no matter how hard he tried, the snow was too deep and the incline too steep. Roy watched with tears in his eyes as his poor horse thrashed at the snow, losing ground with every effort. Coley had been his companion for eight years, and to see him struggle with no help in sight was more than Roy could bear. "Oh, my God," he said out loud. He wasn't a praying man, but the phrase just seemed to come out.

He looked around, quickly scanned the range ahead, looked behind him, not sure what he should do. Somehow he had to get his horse back up on the path and backtrack out of here.

Coley had worn himself out and was still now. Roy sat down and looked at him. His saddle and everything he owned were packed on Coley, along with his Henry rifle. Thinking about the rifle made him reach for the Dragoon at his side. It was gone! He looked below in the snow to see if an impression had been made where it fell out of the holster, but the effort was futile. Even if there was a likely place where it lay, he dare not risk climbing back down for it. It had crossed his mind that he might have to shoot Coley, rather than watch him struggle so hard. But even if he had the Dragoon, he doubted he could do it.

A plan formed in his mind, and as bizarre as it seemed, it was now his only alternative. He hated to leave Coley, but he turned and ran back along the path. As he did so, he kept looking skyward, estimating how much daylight he had left. He moved at a rapid pace, tracing his tracks backward, downward toward where he had come.

After an hour, the first bit of luck struck him. Across the vast expanse toward the east, there they were! The three Indians he had seen earlier! They were three, maybe four miles away, but it appeared they were riding in his direction.

He now kept as close as he could to the treeline, but always kept the three Indians in view. He was now below the snow line and welcomed the solid ground beneath his feet. He quickened his pace even more. It was imperative he keep the three Indians in sight.

For the next hour, he was very careful not to make himself seen, and he now had a chance to rest, since the threesome were still meandering in his direction. It was already becoming dark, and he was sure the Indians would camp somewhere below.

Roy could never remember patience paying off, except in a card game, but now waiting was name of the game. While he watched the progression of the Indians, he let his mind relax and think carefully what his next move would be. They were armed, they had him outgunned, and they certainly knew this area better than he did. But...they also had horses!

***

It had been dark for the better part of three hours. Roy had seen where the three set up camp, in a small hollow with a few trees and some bushes. He had maneuvered himself off to the south a few hundred yards, knowing the slight wind coming down off the Big Horns would draw past him. His movements, as quiet as they were, would not be heard by the men in camp, nor alert the horses. He was in high grass, and there was enough brush to keep him secreted. He had a long time to observe the three. They had built a fire and had roasted something over it. They talked a lot, and he heard laughter from them often. They had blankets, food, and most importantly, a rope strung around four trees to make a corral for the three horses.

He needed that rope and a horse badly. All the while he lay observing the camp, he could not help but think how ironic events had become. Along this trail, it was the Indians who usually lay in wait for the white man, and now the tide had turned. His thoughts kept coming back to Coley, stuck in the snow. He had never felt the kind of sorrow he was now going through, since Coley's existence depended totally upon his actions tonight. And Roy did not know for sure how things would work out.

Another few hours passed, and a chill set in that left him constantly shivering. He had crept to within one hundred yards of the camp, and now he could see the fire was slowly burning out. He hoped the three were asleep, and he hoped they were sound sleepers.

It was time. He inched himself forward, looking up periodically, able to see fairly well in the light of the half moon. He stopped when he was within fifteen yards of the horses. There, before him, the nearest horse, a paint, was looking directly at him. Roy froze in place and continued to observe the paint. In moments the paint returned to eating grass again, his neck dipped over the line that held them in the corral. At least he hadn't spooked, and with a little hope, the other two were equally trained not to spook when someone approached. If these Indians had any pride at all in owning horses, these animals should be well trained.

He had no other choice. On the far side of the corral the fire was nothing but a small glow, and he could see the three men lying near it. He estimated about twenty yards between the horse corral and the campfire. Roy slowly stood up and made his way directly toward the paint. The horse looked back at Roy, but did not move. Now the other two horses turned their heads, and Roy heard a slight nicker from one of them. Then it was quiet again.

Luck was with him. He reached the corral line, walked carefully along it until he reached the paint. So far, so good. He took off his glove and ran a hand along the jaw of the horse, then slid his hand to his neck and patted him. The horse had a light leather line attached, the equivalent of a bridle, very crude, yet very effective. The reins were tied around the horse's neck. He could now see the other two horses were bridled the same way. In an emergency, these Indians could mount and be on their way in seconds. It made complete sense to Roy.

He loosed the reins of the paint, then untied the corral rope, and while leading the paint, he slowly walked around the few trees and coiled up the line as he went. A horse walking in the night never woke up anybody, at least, Roy was counting on that now as he passed in plain sight of the three sleeping Indians.

God forbid anybody should steal another man's horse, he was thinking, but that was exactly what he was doing, and that did not sit well with him. First and foremost in his mind was to return and free Coley as soon as he could...*if* he could..

With the corral line in one hand and leading the paint by the other, Roy Caldwell calmly walked away from the camp. At a safe distance, he swung up on the back of the paint and nudged the horse into a trot. The horse didn't hesitate, he neck-reined easily and responded beautifully to Roy's commands. "You are one good horse," Roy whispered to the paint. "I'd be proud to own you any day."

When he looked back, he could see the other two horses had already strayed from the camp. The Indians would probably spend the first part of the morning trying to round them up. If Roy hadn't had to steal the corral line, they might well believe the horses simply got loose. But with the corral line gone, they would be onto something early. So, time was critical. He had to get back to Coley.

Roy Caldwell trotted the Indian pony up the side of the mountain, and within a couple hours he reached the path. When he was within a hundred yards of where Coley was trapped, he could her him whinny. The Indian pony beneath him responded with a snort.

At the point where Coley had gone down the embankment, Roy dismounted and carefully reviewed his course of action. The rope Roy had stolen was braided leather. It was not near as heavy as a lariat, and Roy did not think it would be strong enough to pull Coley out.

Roy tied one end of the braided leather rope around the pony's neck and tied the other end around his waist. He intended to lower himself down the embankment by use of the leather line. If this horse knew anything about being neck-tied, he wouldn't move. But, if the Indian pony bolted while he was on the way down, at least the paint would pull him back up. He took a firm grip on the line and began to ease himself downward. The snow slipped beneath him, but he kept his footing, and within seconds he reached Coley.

"Easy, old friend," he spoke calmly to Coley as he stroked the side of his neck. Roy loosed the lariat from his saddle and fashioned a loop around Coley's neck. He tied it with a knot that would keep the rope from choking him, yet made the loop small enough so it would not slip over his head.

With Coley secure, Roy then looped the other end of the lariat around his body, gripped the leather line that was tied around the paint's neck above, and pulled himself back up the snow bank. The Indian pony had not budged.

Now came the hard task. With the lariat looped over the paint, Roy simply tugged on the paint's bridle and the pony moved ahead. When the rope was taut, the Indian pony dug in his hooves and pulled steadily ahead. Coley down below knew instinctively he was being helped, and with a fighting effort he began pawing at the drifts, lunging upward, straining every muscle he had to fight his way out of the hole.

The paint pulled easily, calmly as Coley fought to reach higher ground. Within a minute Coley was up on the path. He shook violently and triumphantly stomped his feet. Roy's heart was beating fiercely when he saw his horse on solid ground. He was reasonably sure he could get Coley out, but he had no idea it would happen so quickly. This Indian pony had pulled ever so gently. It was as if he had been specifically trained to do so, as if helping another horse out of a fix was commonplace.

With renewed vigor, Roy coiled up the lariat and the leather line, grabbed both horses by the reins and walked them back along the path. He now realized how light it had become. The sun had been up about an hour already.

Within another fifteen minutes, he was in the open looking down the mountain toward the Bozeman Trail. The sun was blazing on the horizon. He looked toward the draw where the Indian camp was, where he had stolen the horse in the night. He could not see the camp, but he thought he might spot either the Indians or at least the remaining two horses. Nothing was in sight.

It had occurred to him earlier hat he might be able to return the horse before the three woke, but it was way too late now, and far too risky. He had also thought about simply turning the horse loose with the leather line attached. Perhaps the Indians would think the paint simply bolted and hauled the line with him, loosing the other horses. But the line had been tied securely. No Indian would for a moment believe that happened.

And besides, Roy Caldwell had stolen the horse. He didn't intend on keeping it, but the owner of the horse would never understand that. This Indian pony was a wonderful horse, a horse with good demeanor and character, and such a horse and his rider were inseparable. Roy Caldwell understood that better than anyone. So he had to return him.

He thought about all the possessions he had with him. It was not much, but he dug in his bedroll and saddle bags. From them he pulled some beef jerky, three cans of beans, a small bag of coffee and a roll of tobacco. He also removed his knife and scabbard from his belt. All these possessions he placed in a small sack which he secured to the horse's back with the leather corral line.

He could only guess the owner of this horse would have no idea where these gifts came from. That is, assuming this horse made it back to his owner. But it was the least he could do.

Roy tied the bridle around the horse's neck, then gave him a swat on the rear end. The horse started off with a trot down the mountain side. As he did so, Roy swung up into his saddle and watched the paint. Then, the Indian horse slowed, turned, and trotted back toward Roy. "What the hell?" he was thinking. Was this horse coming back to him? It did return, but it trotted right by him and stopped no more than twenty yards away.

It was then Roy Caldwell spotted the three Indians, and he broke into a cold sweat. The threesome and the other two horses stood on an embankment above the paint no more than another twenty or thirty yards away. Roy Caldwell had just walked beneath them a few minutes ago. Certainly he had been within range of their arrows. In fact, he was now.

And then he realized, from where they now stood they had a clear view of the ridge where he and Coley had tried to cross the Big Horns. He was sure they had witnessed the ordeal as he freed his horse, and they must have realized why he needed the paint. Even now, as he looked up at them, the three remained standing, their bows over their heads, not threatening to any degree.

Roy simply stared at the three for another several seconds while one of the men worked his way down the embankment to the paint. He grabbed the reins, and in a smooth movement he mounted the horse.

Roy reached up and touched his hat as a friendly gesture. The Indian, dressed splendidly in buckskin attire, nodded back.

Roy turned his horse and trotted off toward Fort Smith. He was tired, and so was Coley, but he knew he'd be there by nightfall.

* * *

LYDIA PEARLMAN

It had all seemed like a great adventure for Lydia Pearlman. The territory west of the Mississippi had been open for several years. Towns were springing up out of nowhere, mostly at the confluence of mighty rivers, others emerging on the open plains or along mountain streams in the depth of the Rockies. Those were the mining towns, which often times sprang up with the best intentions of becoming the capital of a not yet named state. In almost all cases they became nothing more than ghost towns, or at most, non-thriving towns of just a few buildings. The remaining inhabitants usually consisted of a handful of people who had reached the end of the road.

That's what Lydia was thinking about as she sat in her room overlooking the almost deserted street below. A slight rumble interrupted the silence, and a few seconds later the stagecoach rolled past, then went out of view. It stopped, she was sure, in front of the hotel down the street.

Lydia's gaze once again focused on the street below. It was as if she were in a trance, so pensive were her thoughts. She had been reviewing the circumstances under which she ended up in Miles City. Some ten years back when she was sixteen, her father had been killed in a barroom brawl. She never knew who her mother was, and the only living relative was an aunt on her father's side. Though Lydia had never met her, the woman said Lydia could live with her. There really was no other choice at the time, so Lydia looked upon the move from the East to St. Louis as an adventure. St. Louis, was, after all, the then western-most thriving city on the Mississippi.

The city had its attractions, but she fell into hard times. Barely three months had passed when her aunt died of consumption, leaving nothing of any monetary value behind. Lydia continued to work in a laundry, then did part time sewing, and for several months worked in a dry goods store as a clerk.

She was not a particularly good-looking woman, or so she had learned over the years. There were many potential suitors in St. Louis, and though her intentions of moving to this river city were not originally to find a husband, she discovered the men did not find her as interesting or exciting as other women. The suitors had been few. She at one time had what she considered a relationship. The man was a trapper by trade, and although he said he would marry her when he returned from his next trip, he never did return. She had waited three years for him and never learned whether he had been killed, or whether he never returned because he did not wish to fulfill his commitment.

Sometime later she had entered into a business arrangement with a gambler by the name of Louis Mardan. He wanted her to accompany him north on a Mississippi steamer into "new gambling territory," as he had put it. It was to be her duty to handle his financial affairs. What he really wanted was a woman on his arm, someone to spot rich drunks who had nothing better to do with their money, but lose it to a two-bit gambler whose only means of acquiring wealth was by cheating at cards. Cheating a drunk was so much easier than cheating a respectable gambler, Louis had once told her.

She had tried to accommodate Louis, but it was not in her nature to cheat people out of money. Of course, Louis justified his trade by maintaining that if a person played cards while he was drunk he deserved to lose his money.

After two weeks on the steamer, and just short of the Dakota Territory, one of Louis' drunks shot him dead at the card table. There were enough witnesses to testify Louis had cheated, so at Yankton, the next stop, his body was dropped off at the pier.

The Captain had also thrown Lydia off the steamer and made it known to the authorities, that this woman was nothing more than a thief and should be treated as such.

Word spread rapidly, and in time the only work she could find was in gambling houses. At first her job was simply to push drinks for the proprietor, or line up the men with the soiled doves that worked on the upper floor. It was not long before she too became one of the ladies of the night.

Any young girl that was new in such a house immediately drew attention, and although the thought of sleeping with just anybody off the street was repulsive, Lydia eventually succumbed to the profession. At first, she had spent time with professional people such as bankers and merchants and retailers. These were men who gained entrance to the parlor through a back door. Most of these prominent businessmen were daytime clients. The nighttime clients were much rowdier, usually cowboys or soldiers passing through, headed up to the western border of the Dakota Territory. They were a lowly lot, prone to cussing and fighting, and on so many occasions, skipping out without paying.

There was a time, she remembered, when she honestly believed that some man would eventually enter her life, who wanted her for who she was, rather than what she was. In due time she understood that it was simply the pleasure of a few minutes that the men wanted. Their desires consisted of nothing more than a respite from their boring and mundane lives at work or at home. In any case she accommodated them, and she had learned how to tease men, how to get an extra tip out of them that the Madame downstairs did not know about.

That worked for some time, and Lydia Pearlman, who had become known as simply *Pearl*, had put away a goodly sum of money. It was money no one else, not even any of the other girls around her, knew about.

But one day the Madame entered her room without knocking and discovered Lydia in the process of putting away a canister filled with tip money. One of her guards ransacked Lydia's room, beat her and tossed her out on the street.

Luckily, Lydia had the bulk of her extra cash secreted in a shack behind the brothel. She procured the money that evening, and the next day she found a merchant going north on a freighter and paid him to take her along.

Such had been her life for the past decade. She had moved from one town to another somehow believing that a new environment would produce a new beginning. In all that time, not once had she ever met a man of any class who was interested in her except for the pleasure of paid company. Rarely had she found anyone she could trust, and even if she did, circumstance always forced her to move on. What had started out to be an adventure so many years ago had somehow ended up dragging her into a life of despair and loneliness.

Lydia Pearlman gazed out onto the street again and suddenly burst into tears. "My god," she sobbed. "What have I done to myself?"

There was a light rap at her door. "Pearl?" the voice outside called out.

She composed herself as best she could, but kept her face toward the street. "Yes, come in." She had recognized the voice of Jessie, the bartender downstairs.

He stuck his head in. "Sam is asking for you."

Sam was the hotel owner. He was an occasional client, always polite with her, and perhaps one of the best of the lot she accommodated. She tried to gain her composure and said, "Tell Sam to give me a few minutes, and then send him up."

"Sam's not here, Pearl. He sent word from the hotel you should come. Said it was important."

She turned around, and Jessie saw her flushed face. "You all right, Miss Pearl?"

"I'm fine. I'm fine. Thank you."

Jessie closed the door and she listened for a moment as his

light footsteps trailed off down the hall. Sam periodically came to see her, but not once had she ever gone over to the hotel to accommodate him. "It wouldn't be proper," he had once said. "Not with boarders about."

But the hotel didn't have many boarders these days. Perhaps Sam had changed his mind. Lydia dressed herself appropriately, applied some makeup to her face and went downstairs onto the street. The stagecoach was still in front of the hotel, and a few people had gathered out front. She made her way past the small crowd into the lobby of the hotel. Sam was usually somewhere nearby, but he was not present at the moment. She approached the clerk behind the counter.

He was expecting her. "Sam's in room 205. He said to send you right up."

That was strange, she thought. She glanced about the room. A few familiar faces were present, most turned aside now. One gentleman, whom she knew regularly, simply raised his newspaper in front of his face. This was not the normal course for Lydia to be entering a hotel, especially in the daytime.

Everyone in the room knew who Lydia was, and what she did for a living. But she did not care, since over the years she had grown accustomed to being shunned from society. She went straight to the stairs and walked up quickly and located the room. When she entered, Sam was sitting on a chair beside the bed. In the bed, and fully clothed, was a young woman not unlike herself, dark-haired and rather slim of build.

"Pearl," said Sam. "I'm glad you came. This girl just arrived on the stage. She's very sick. Someone's trying to locate Doc Burns."

Lydia stood silently for a moment. "Why did you ask for me?"

"I was going to send for Dolly, but then I remembered she was in Forsythe." Dolly was the Madame of the parlor where Lydia worked. "So then I sent for you," Sam went on. "Nobody seems to know much about her. We assumed she was going to work with you girls at the parlor."

"No," said Lydia. "We weren't expecting a new girl."

The young lady on the bed opened her eyes and slowly turned her head toward Lydia. Lydia placed her hand on her forehead. She was burning with a fever.

"Get me some cold water, Sam. This girl needs immediate attention." Sam hustled out the door, and as soon as he was gone, Lydia rolled the young lady over on her side as gently as she could and began unlacing the back of her dress. The girl needed the comfort of loose fitting clothes, something that would allow her to breathe easier. Lydia dabbed at her sweaty forehead with a towel. Sam came in with a pitcher of water and filled a wash basin. Lydia drenched the towel and continued to dab the forehead of the young lady, then loosed her bodice and again cooled her skin with the damp towel.

"Am I going to die?" the young lady asked faintly.

"No, you're not going to die," Lydia calmed her. The girl's eyes were glazed now.

Sam looked on and explained that the stagecoach driver said the young lady took ill a few days back, and that he advised her then she should get off the stage and seek a doctor. But the lady had refused.

Doc Burns entered the room carrying his satchel and came straight to the bedside. He touched her forehead, reached under her dress and felt her legs, turned her over and ran a hand down inside the unlaced dress.

He looked at Lydia. "Help me get her clothes off." He turned to Sam. "Get me a tub of cold water right now. This lady is burning up."

Lydia and Doc Burns worked furiously to remove her outer clothes and her laced shoes until she lay clad only in her undergarments. Then they continued to soak her with wet towels. Two men came in carrying a tin bathtub and placed it at the head of the bed. Soon, more help came through the door, filling the tub with buckets of cold water.

The young lady opened her eyes again and looked at Lydia and mouthed something. Lydia bent down to hear what she was saying.

"Please...tell him...I'm sorry," she said weakly.

"Tell who?" asked Lydia. Her eyes were now staring, as if unseeing.

"Henry," she answered.

Two more men came in with buckets of cold water and poured them into the tub and ran out for more.

"Let's get her into the tub," Doc burns instructed. He motioned for Sam and Lydia to help him, then suddenly stopped. He leaned down and put his ear on her breast for some time, then looked up and slowly eased himself back into his chair. He gave a heavy sigh. "She had the fever for too long. There was nothing we could do for her." He slowly pulled a sheet up to her neckline and looked at the white, fleshy face. "Young thing, too," he said.

The two men carrying the water entered the room again, looked at the girl on the bed, and when they saw Doc shake his head, they too left the room.

"Who is she?" asked the Doc.

"Don't know," said Sam. "Might be some identification in her bag."

Doc Burns stood up, put his coat back on and picked up his satchel. "I'll get hold of Jacobson and tell him we got a body over here that needs to be buried." He looked at Sam. "If we can find out who she is and where she came from, I suppose we ought to send a wire to the next of kin."

"Poor thing," Doc Burns said as he looked again into the dead girl's face. "And so young." He left the room.

"Pearl," said Sam. "I'd appreciate it if maybe you'd kind of look through her things. I'll have them sent up."

Lydia agreed. When Sam was gone, she looked into the face of the girl. There was nothing spectacular about her looks. Rather plain, dark hair like herself, perhaps a little slimmer in build, and about the same age. Lydia could not help but wonder what sort of life this lady had lived up to this point. Did she have a profession? And what was her reason for coming to Miles City?

Lydia looked again at the girl. If there were only some way she could learn anything from this pale, lifeless face. Lydia's gaze focused on the dress, which she had worn, now draped over an adjoining chair. She moved the dress aside to expose a small purse.

She opened the bag and began to sort through the contents. It contained a mirror and some facial powder, along with eighteen dollars and some small change. In a small leather case Lydia discovered a letter of credit from a bank in Chicago. It was made out in the name of Sally Sommerfield. It was for the amount of fifty dollars, and had obviously been cashed, as indicated by the bank stamp.

Also in the leather case was a series of tickets. Lydia thumbed through them one by one. This girl had come from Chicago to Bismarck, the end of the railroad line, then from Bismarck to Miles City by stagecoach.

What Lydia found most interesting was that Miles City was not her end destination. The tickets continued on to Bearcreek Junction, Montana Territory. Lydia had no idea where that was, or how far it was.

Sam came into the bedroom carrying two bags, which he set down at the foot of the bed. "Find out anything, Pearl?"

"Yes," said Lydia as she placed the contents back into the purse. "Her name is Sally Sommerfield, from Chicago. There's no address, but there's a canceled bank note and eighteen dollars in cash."

Sam simply shook his head. "Just about enough to bury her and send a wire back. Poor girl. I wonder if she had any family back home."

Lydia was quiet for some time, and then said. "I wonder too."

Jacobson, a little man in stature, entered the room and removed his hat in respect for the dead girl. He was very efficient at his job and quite often directly to the point.

"I understand she is a newcomer to Miles City," he said.

"Yes," answered Sam.

"Is there money enough to pay for her funeral?"

"There's enough," said Sam.

Satisfied with Sam's answer, Jacobson unraveled a heavy quilt he had under his arm and proceeded to maneuver it under the girl. He wrapped her securely and had Sam help carry her downstairs to his waiting buggy.

At eleven o'clock the next morning, Jacobson had already dug a grave and had her body hauled to the gravesite. The only people in attendance were Jacobson, Sam, Doc Burns and Lydia. Doc Burns offered to say a few words, which didn't amount to much, other than he hoped the Lord would accept her into his arms.

Ten dollars covered the funeral costs, and a few dollars more covered the cost to send a wire back to Chicago.

For the next three days, Lydia sat in her room above the parlor, spending most of her hours simply staring out onto the street. She had been asked to entertain clients, but had refused, easily understood when she simply said it was her time of the month.

And while she was looking out onto the street, the stage from Glendive rolled past, an hour behind schedule. As soon as it was out of view, Lydia turned to look at the display on her bed. Three dresses were neatly laid out, along with other wearing apparel. They belonged to Sally Sommerfield and had been given to her by Sam. There was no use sending the clothes back, he said, and Doc Burns had agreed. She had tried on all three dresses. They were plain, for the most part, but each fit her quite well.

Early the next morning, when the stagecoach left for Forsythe, Lydia Pearlman was on it.

***

It was a long trip. She had no idea where Bearcreek Junction was, and it made no difference, because she had already decided that somewhere between Miles City and the final destination, she would get off the coach. She had used the ticket purchased by Sally

Sommerfield, which had been accepted by the stagecoach driver without question. The stage had left at daybreak, a time when Sam was at breakfast, like he always was. Hardly anyone else was on the street, so it was an easy departure. And she had no remorse leaving the town. Like all the towns before, it had offered her nothing. What lay ahead of her she did not know, nor did she care. Every few hours, the stage stopped to change the horse team. At the end of the first day, she had traveled eighty miles, she guessed, and had overnighted in a station that was far short of comfort.

On the second day, a man in the coach had pointed out a landmark known as Pompey's Pillar, a formation named by Lewis and Clark. She had no knowledge of it, only knew that on occasion the Yellowstone River appeared off to the north. She considered it a grand river, so very blue and pure and wide, and so belonging to this vast landscape of green. She could not believe how far she could see at any given moment. It seemed the horizon was thousands of miles away, and then almost magically the coach seemed to be emerged in rolling hills, and then came the huge expanses again.

On more than one occasion, Indians had been spotted riding on ridges parallel to the stage road. It was nothing to be alarmed about, the driver had informed her. No need to worry ever since the Battle of the Little Bighorn. She had heard of the man called Custer, and that he and his men had been wiped out completely by the Indians at this battle, which had taken place only a few years back. Given the fact that all of Custer's men were dead, she did not quite understand why she should not worry. Yet, none of the other passengers in the coach seemed alarmed. Someone mentioned the battlefield was somewhere off to the south of them at that point. The best part of that day was when the passengers had an overnighter in Billings, in quite good accommodations with good food.

The next day, the stage continued along the Yellowstone, but in a southerly direction. Every few hours, the stage stopped for fresh horses, but the stops were nothing more than a log cabin with a corral that held the change for the new team. Finally, at a place called

Clark's Fork, she inquired where the next town was.

"Cody, ma'am," the driver had answered. Won't be there until late tomorrow." Lydia had never heard of the city, but she decided she would get off there.

During the entire trip, Lydia Pearlman had contained her conversation. The passengers had varied from day to day. Some getting on, others getting off. Now, since Billings, the same four men were riding in the coach. Not once, she suddenly realized, had another woman ridden in the coach since she left Miles City. But the one thing she discovered and very much appreciated, was how polite every man on the coach had been to her. It had been so long since she had been treated with respect, that she hardly knew how to react.

She studied the faces of the four men, almost afraid to initiate conversation, but she finally did. "What do people do for a living around here?"

"Mostly ranch country, some mining," an older man offered.

"Some people trap for a living," said another.

For an instant, Lydia's thoughts flashed back to St. Louis when she had once been in love with a trapper. A trapper who never returned. It almost took her breath away to recollect, at least for a moment, how it had once felt to be loved.

The coach moved on into a flat, almost desert like countryside. Yet, toward the west, she could see the foothills that rolled up to the mountains. It was a marvel how often the landscape changed, and each time the view presented her with a new sense of beauty.

She felt a real comfort riding with these men. Somehow, she knew, the death of that girl back in Miles City, as morbid as it seemed, was a moment in time that might well change her destiny.

She sat back, not minding the hard bench seat, nor the bumps and juggling from side to side. And she had never felt better in her life.

Then, she realized the stagecoach was slowing, and she peered out expecting to see another change station. But there was none. The stagecoach jerked to a halt, and the driver stepped down from the seat and opened the door. "This is Bearcreek Junction, Ma'am."

She looked across the plains into the vast expanse where a dirt trail led off toward the west and disappeared over a hill. She could see in every direction for several miles, yet there was nothing in sight to indicate that anyone inhabited this land.

"Ma'am?" asked the driver again as he offered her his hand.

She stepped down from the coach to the ground and once again looked about. The other men in the coach also departed, simply to stretch their legs. The driver seemed concerned as he climbed back to the driver's seat, then to the top of the coach where he scanned the horizon in all directions.

"You expecting somebody, Ma'am?" one of the men asked her.

She looked him directly in the face, unable to give an answer. She felt panic inside her. This was Bearcreek Junction? What had Sally Sommerfield hoped to do here? Why had a ticket taken her to this destination, a crossroads that seemed to lead to nowhere?

"Someone's coming!" the driver hollered as he pointed off toward the west.

Everyone turned to where he was pointing. Dust swirled upwards in the calm of the afternoon. Someone or something was coming on at a fast pace. They all watched patiently until a figure of some sort began to form on the horizon. From two miles away, everyone watched as a buggy, drawn by a tall and stout horse, eventually broke the top of a rise. The rig descended toward them at a continued clip.

Within a few minutes the buggy pulled to a halt before the stage, and the man driving it stepped to the ground. He was tall, dressed in a neat black suit with a white shirt and a black string tie. He came a few steps closer, and when he removed his hat she could see how wavy his hair was. Long brown locks reached almost to his shoulders, and he had a thick, brown mustache to match. She thought him to be about forty, and she also thought him to be one of the most handsome men she had ever seen.

"Miss Sommerfield?" he asked. He was standing about ten feet away.

She stared at him, unable to respond.

"I'm Henry Stouter," he said.

Henry? she thought to herself. That was the name Sally Sommerfield had mentioned before she died!

He seemed puzzled. "You are Miss Sommerfield, are you not?"

The question stunned her. "Y-yes," she answered. "I am."

When he smiled a few deep wrinkles broke his tanned face. "You are more beautiful than I ever imagined."

She could hardly believe what she just heard right here before this small crowd of onlookers. The passengers, if not stunned, were certainly curious about the drama unfolding before them.

Finally the stage driver broke the silence. "I'll get your bags, ma'am." He handed them down to the other men on the ground, who carried them to the buggy. "Let's go," he hollered at the passengers. When they were inside, the driver whistled and snapped his reins.

The rumble of the stagecoach wheels was out of earshot before Henry Stouter spoke.

"This is, I'm sure, sort of awkward for both of us."

"Yes," she said, not at all sure what she was responding to.

"You had a nice trip? I imagine it was long, and you must be tired."

"No. Yes," she said changing her mind. "That is, the trip was long, but I'm not tired."

He nodded and let out a slight laugh. She liked his laugh, liked his smile. When he offered to help her up onto the buckboard, she felt how callused his hand was, but what struck her most was how gentle and polite this man appeared.

"We've all been waiting for you," he said. "Of course, I want you to be comfortable with everything." She could tell he was searching for words, and she gave him all the time he needed.

"Well," he went on. "I want you to meet all the hands and

get the feel of the ranch. And then, if you still agree to the arrangement, well, then, maybe in a week or two we can go to Cody..." He stopped for a moment, and then quickly finished. "And be married proper."

When she turned to look at him, she was sure her mouth was gaping.

He went on. "You said in your letter you thought you would like the wide open country. You still feel that way?"

Her wide eyes and broad smile answered for him. She looked about. She had never seen so much green at one time. The mountain peaks to the west rose upward as if they would never end. She had never seen mountains like this before. It was a new and fascinating beauty.

"Can you cook?" he asked.

"Some," she answered."

He laughed. "Anything would be better than what we drum up." He looked at her. "I hope you like it here. The ranch ain't much, but it's growing, and it sure can use a pretty woman's touch."

She loved his chiseled smile, and she loved the way he spoke. Not hesitating, she edged closer and grabbed him firmly by the arm.

Henry Stouter snapped the reins and set the horse into an easy lope.

***

MAN OF TEETH

Back at the Doan Store, they had told him to follow the Western Cattle Trail until he came to the Elm Fork off of the Red. From there, the Wichita Agency was no more than a day's ride to the northeast across Oklahoma Territory. That route was not recommended since it was inhabited by the Commanches, a tribe that did not tolerate any infringement on their land. They recommended he keep going north until he struck the Washita, and then back track along that river to the agency. That, however, was an extra two-day ride.

The Wichita Agency was where young Augustus was headed. He had just crossed a river, but he wasn't sure which one, since unfortunately the only map he had was in his head. He had ridden north a day and a half, which should have placed him either at the North Fork of the Red, or could this possibly be the Washita?

No, this was the North Fork or the Elm Fork off of the Red. He halted his red roan, stood in the stirrups and looked around as if the extra few inches in height would give him a better idea of his location. The land was rolling plains, barren as far as he could see. To the north, a vague line of darkness like a set of mountains strung across the horizon, but on close inspection he guessed it might well be a set of storm clouds. Yet it did not feel like rain.

"Saber," he said to his horse. "I don't know where we are for sure. You got any suggestions?" Augustus slouched back in his saddle, and when he did so, his horse started walking in a northeast direction.

"They told us not to cross Commanche land," he said to his horse. "But with nightfall coming, we might be all right."

He had heard that Indians did not attack at night, and it would be dark within an hour. If he hustled his horse along, he should reach the Wichita Agency by early morning.

He urged his horse into a trot, an easy pace he knew Saber could handle. He kept to the lower side of the hills, picking, whenever he could, a draw that kept him out of sight for the most part. He constantly scanned the hilltops around him, hoping to catch sight of Indians if they did appear, and hopeful he would spot them before they spotted him.

The arrival of night gave him a sense of security. He had reduced his horse to a walk, since now it was too dark to see a clear trail ahead. Lucky for him his horse had good night vision.

They plodded on into the dark, and somewhere near midnight Augustus found himself dozing in the saddle.

A sudden, cool breeze awakened him, a warning that a change in weather was upon him. Now, even with his eyes fully open, he could not see a thing in front of him. Clouds had moved in, bringing a northern, he feared. He no sooner got his slicker on when the rain whipped over the plains in a fierce charge of indifference.

The wind was relentless, charging at him full force, the rain coming so hard it stung his face. His slicker whipped about him like a torn sail in a heavy gale as he jammed his hat down over his forehead, holding it with one hand, gripping his reins tight with the other. Augustus cursed himself. There was no respite from this blowing force, not here out in the open.

Then, as if by magic, lightning tore across the sky with a streak so long, it lit up the area like daylight. The few seconds of brightness gave Augustus just enough time to glimpse some treetops in a draw off to his right.

"Come on, Saber." He spurred his horse and headed down a slight incline, the lightning bursts occasionally showing him the way. In short time, he reached the draw strewn with trees and bushes thick enough to grant him some shelter. He climbed off his horse and led him into the trees, allowing the lightning to show him the way. At the bottom, a gushing creek snaked its way into the black. Near the edge of the water, Augustus found a high bank and a ledge that granted a reprieve from the wind and rain.

He loosed the cinch on his saddle to give his horse a breather. Exhausted and tired, he squatted down and huddled against the clay wall, thankful for this small bit of comfort. He wished he could build a fire, but he knew there would not be a dry twig for fifty miles around, so he resolved himself to the fact he would have to sit out the rain. He shuddered from the cold, inched himself closer to the protection of the clay wall. As soon as the rain quit he would move on.

That was his intention, but inside of five minutes he was fast asleep.

He awoke a few hours later, startled by the incessant yammering of a half dozen crows in a nearby tree. When he stood, the crows flushed in unison and sailed off into a dismal and damp fog. The air was so heavy and thick, Augustus could see no more than fifty feet.

The hoof prints of his horse led off down the draw, and within a few minutes Augustus located him grazing on some bottom grass. Augustus pulled some hard tack from his saddlebag and munched on it as he tightened up the cinch. Once in the saddle, he followed the bottom along the swift running creek. After a half mile, he found a flat area where it looked like he could cross. The bottom was laden with rocks, which his horse picked through nicely, and once on the other side Augustus nudged him up a steep bank.

Saber stretched upward easily, but just short of the rise the entire bank broke away. Saber lost his footing and tumbled backward throwing Augustus from the saddle. In seconds the two rolled back down the embankment, tumbling end over end. Augustus managed to grab on to some brush, breaking his fall, but his horse continued downward and slammed on the rocks below. Augustus scrambled down to the animal, fearing the worst. He managed to get Saber to his feet, grabbed his reins and pulled at him to get him on the bank. Saber finally limped out of the water and stood, his back foot lifted off the ground.

"Damn," said Augustus as he examined the leg. It was broke just below the hock. "Oh, God, now what?"

There was no other choice. Saber's head hung low, his eyes betraying the pain he was in. Augustus loosed the cinch and pulled the saddle and blanket from him, then released the bridle. With tears welling up in his eyes, he cocked the hammer on his revolver. If there were Indians in the area, they were sure to hear the shot, but his horse was suffering. The blast echoed along the creek and Saber was down.

Augustus sat and for the next few minutes cried his heart out.

When his head cleared he began to assess the situation. A thought had barely entered his mind when he heard a crashing noise from up river. Through the fog, four deer came directly at him and ran past only a few feet away. In seconds they were out of sight.

Something had scared them, Augustus realized. He pulled his Sharp's rifle from the scabbard, grabbed a box of shells from his saddlebag and stuffed them in his coat. He got his hat, and in moments was running as best he could through the water. He dare not leave any tracks behind just in case it was Indians who had scared the deer.

He had just reached a bend in the creek when he first heard the splashing water behind him. Three Indians on ponies stopped where his dead horse lay. One of them dropped from his horse and began to examine the saddle. He commanded something to the others, who raced up and over the same bank he and Saber had tried to ascend.

Augustus listened carefully until the sound of the hoof beats disappeared. It occurred to him he might get a lucky shot at the remaining Indian, grab his horse and head out. No sooner had that thought crossed his mind, when the Indian mounted his horse and slowly began walking in his direction, his eyes skirting the banks.

Augustus couldn't just shoot him in cold blood, he decided, and he also knew he couldn't stay in the water without making noise. He crawled onto the bank and carefully and quickly made his way through the brush and trees. If he could stay far enough ahead in the fog, he might be able to gain some ground. If he could reach the upper bank unseen, it was just possible he could find his way into another draw and evade the Indians altogether.

The instinct to keep moving was a driving force as he clambered up the bank to the top. He turned long enough to glimpse the Indian below in the fog, still moving slowly through the creek bottom. So far, so good.

He took off on a dead run across the hills, his eyes searching, looking, scanning every rise, every bush. Off to his left now, he was sure he had seen some movement. Horses? Indians on horses?

Then, to his right a faint outline of riders began to appear. He was still running as fast as he could. A dog barked faintly from somewhere ahead. Suddenly huge spires formed, like church steeples. Augustus stopped running and looked about him. Indians on horseback seemed to have magically encircled him, and now, as he studied his surroundings he realized he was standing at the outskirts of an Indian village!

The Indians on their ponies were on the move, forming a circle about him. He whirled about, his whole being shaking, terrified at what he was seeing.

And then, from somewhere he heard the closeness of hoof beats. He turned just in time to see the oncoming rider, and though he made an attempt to raise the Sharp's rifle, his reaction was far too late. A war club caught him on the side of the head and sent him spinning to the ground. Whoops and blood curdling cries were the last sounds he heard.

When he woke, his head was splitting, the surroundings spinning. Slowly the inside of the tent came into focus. A small fire sent swirls of smoke upward, and beyond the fire was a young Indian lady who appeared to be sewing. She was sitting cross-legged, dressed in fine buckskin attire. She noticed he was awake and hollered something in her native tongue, but obviously not at him. Immediately a tall Indian man entered through the flap of the tent. He stared at Augustus, his glare alone enough to unnerve the insides of the bravest. Seconds later, four more Indians entered. All sat about the fire cross-legged and looked directly at him. He was shaking uncontrollably.

The young lady approached him with a cup of water, and although Augustus' throat was dry, he was suspicious of the offer, sure it was poisoned. He thought for certain this crowd was going to watch him choke and gag until the life was cursed out of him. She must have read his suspicions, since she sipped the water and then offered it to him once more. Augustus gulped it down.

The girl returned to her place, and now the men, all older except for the first man who entered the tent, began chatting among themselves, none of the language remotely familiar to Augustus. If he could read any body language, it appeared the youngest warrior was most hostile. His voice was louder, fiercer than the rest. Occasionally an elder man would calm him with a few words, and after one of the elders apparently had heard enough from the younger, he made a gesture that indicated the brave should shut up, and he did.

The leader of the group was an old man with wrinkles in his face deep enough to hold a silver dollar. A long scar creased the top of his forehead, which Augustus guessed was a war wound. His jaw was swollen immensely on one side as if he had been recently struck with a club. The swelling was obviously painful to the man, since he often ran his tongue along the inside of his mouth and occasionally pressed on the outside of his jaw with gentle, but old fingers. He motioned to the girl.

"I am Lone Grass." She said to Augustus.

Augustus sat up, stunned that she could speak English.

"How is your name?" she asked.

"Augustus."

She turned to the older man and said something in her native tongue. All the men nodded their heads.

"Are you Commanche?" Augustus asked.

"Yes." She pointed to the oldest. "He is Chief Kills Many. He is the leader of our village, a medicine man."

"How is it you speak such good English?" asked Augustus.

"My father was a white man."

The medicine man spoke to her and she interpreted. "Chief Kills Many asks why you cross Commanche territory."

"I'm on my way to the Wichita Agency."

She interpreted again. "If you go to the agency, why were you going south and not north? our Chief asks."

"I was lost," he answered. "I'm not as good with directions as an Indian."

When she interpreted, all the men managed to grunt out a laugh, even the younger brave who at first appeared so hostile.

The younger one asked a question and motioned for Lone Grass to speak for him.

"Young Bear asks why you threatened him with your rifle."

It was clear now. Young Bear, the warrior, was the one who had clubbed him. "Would Young Bear not do the same if surrounded by white men?"

When she interpreted his words, all the elders again grunted their approval with the answer. Lone Grass asked why he had shot his horse. Did he not realize a report that loud would alarm anyone in the area?

"I thought about it," Augustus answered, "He had a broken leg and I could not see my horse suffer any more. We were together for seven years."

She relayed his answer to the council members, who nodded, indicating they seemed to understand.

For several seconds it was silent in the tent, and then Chief Kills Many produced a book from a parfleche that hung at his side and handed it to Augustus. It was one of the books he had been carrying in his saddlebags.

Lone Grass spoke. "Our Chief wants to know if you can read the white man's tongue."

Augustus stared at the old man, then opened to the first page of the dime novel that glorified the exploits of a gunfighter. He began reading. "When the train ceased movement at the Arborville station, a stately gentleman clad in fine attire emerged onto the platform and surmised his surroundings with the eyes of an eagle. Those in close proximity recognized him as the Kid by his broad shoulders and his smooth hands that were used to handling the six guns that adorned each side of his hips." Augustus looked up.

The circle of Indians was nodding their heads. A few words were exchanged among them, and in moments all had left the tent.

Augustus sat mystified. "What will they do to me?" he asked.

"They are discussing that at the moment. Are you hungry?"

"What time is it?"

"It is evening. You have been resting for a day. Are you hungry?"

He nodded, not sure what his fate was to be. She offered him some flat bread and a mixture of some sort as hard as hardtack, but tastier. A few strips of jerky accompanied the meal, which he ate heartily.

"Young Bear is my half brother," she offered. "He is a good warrior, but does not have patience like Chief Kills Many. Patience is a skill, which one must acquire. It is not given at birth. Do you agree?"

Augustus nodded, not sure he knew what she was getting at.

"You too, must be patient while the chiefs decide. Tonight you will remain here, but do not attempt to leave the camp. There are many braves outside watching."

Augustus said nothing, his face still steeped in mystery concerning his fate.

She read his face. "So far, you are in favor. You answered well, and it is good that you can read."

"Why is that?" he inquired.

"If all goes well, you will discover why in the morning."

At that moment her brother, Young Bear, returned and sat near the fire. Lone Grass prepared food for him, and as he ate, he never once took his eyes off of Augustus.

When morning came, Young Bear was in the same position as the night before. Lone Grass was busy at her sewing, and the fire was still burning.

"I must relieve myself," Augustus said to her.

She spoke to Young Bear, and he motioned for Augustus to come with him.

Outside the tent, the morning sun was a brilliant glow on the horizon. A chill hovered in the air, but a comfortable one. Young Bear led him to a draw behind the camp where he relieved himself. The village consisted of about 25 teepees, and as he walked back to Young Bear's tent, those who were up and about eyed him suspiciously, especially the children who probably had never seen a blond haired individual. He suspected his canvas pants and red suspenders were equally mystifying to the onlookers.

When he returned to the teepee, Lone Grass had a thick soup cooking over a fire. He thought he would be restricted to the interior of the tent, but Young Bear did not indicate he should enter, so he sat on the ground next to the soup kettle, which gave off an excellent aroma. As he looked over the campsite, he could not help but wonder what Lone Grass meant the night before when she said it was in his favor that he could read. He had conjured up in his mind that he would be scalped or tied to a post and burned alive, but he was beginning to feel a sense of comfort by his captors, if indeed, he was a captive. What else would he be under the circumstances? Other than the lump on the side of his head, he was feeling pretty good.

He suddenly spotted his saddlebags lying near the tent. Young Bear had probably taken possession of them. The saddle and bridle were nowhere around. He figured one of the Indians had claimed them, and he was sure he would never see them again.

He was thinking about Saber, his horse, when a shadow appeared on the ground next to him. He looked up to see Chief Kills Many standing before him. With him were the same three council members who had visited the night before. The Chief held firm to his lance with all the feathers and scalps he had acquired over his long life. The lance seemed to serve more as a crutch now, rather than an affirmation of his heroic deeds. In his other hand he carried a small wooden box. Kills Many spoke to Lone Grass in Commanche, and when he finished he handed the box to her and asked her to interpret for him.

"Kills Many asks if you know what these instruments are," Lone Grass said.

Augustus opened the lid. The box contained an assortment of shiny metallic hand tools with strangely shaped heads. He had never seen such tools before but he guessed from their strange shapes and silvery finish that they were instruments used by a doctor or a dentist. A closer examination revealed their bloody purpose.

"Tell Kills Many these are tools for removing teeth."

She interpreted for him, and then, "Kills Many asks if you can use these tools."

"Where did he get them?"

Lone Grass eyed the medicine man, then spoke to Augustus. "I know where they came from. I think it is better you do not ask."

Augustus looked at the old man with the swollen face. "I am not a dentist," he finally said. Lone Grass did not understand the word dentist. "I am not a man of teeth," Augustus clarified.

She told Kills Many what Augustus said, and the Chief reiterated that Augustus maintained he could read the white man's language.

Augustus nodded.

Kills Many pulled a pamphlet from the side of the case. It was a description of all the tools and directions for their use.

Kills Many said something to Lone Grass, and then assumed a sitting position on a stump near the tent. The other sub chiefs sat on the ground, waiting, their patience in full force.

"Kills Many says you read and he will wait," said Lone Grass.

"Good Lord!" said Augustus. "I don't know anything about teeth. Tell him, I am not a man of teeth."

Kills Many remained planted on the stump like a stone, one hand on each knee, his gaze straight ahead. It was apparent he would not move. Augustus stared at the pamphlet. It was one thing to read directions, but it was another thing to use the instruments.

For the better part of an hour Augustus sat on the ground reading over the pamphlet and examining the instruments. Kills Many did not move, nor did any of his friends, which included Young Bear whose stoic posture presented a formidable force. It was now quite apparent why it was important that Augustus could read. If he did not comply with Chief Kills Many's request, he might well be adding his scalp to the Chief's lance.

He skipped the first few pages since they applied to filling teeth, a skill he could not remotely deliver. After reading the successive pages several times he kept coming back to a recurring phrase—*In most cases, extracting the tooth will solve the problem.*

Feeling totally helpless, Augustus finally approached Kills Many. When he asked the Chief to open his mouth, the old man grimaced, but did as he was told. Augustus slipped a thumb in alongside the gum and pressed on the last molar on the infected side of his jaw. Kills Many grunted heavily, and though he raised his rear-end off the stump, he kept his hands firmly planted on his knees. Augustus could not help but admire the old man's courage.

"Abscess," he said out loud. It was one of several new words he had picked up from reading the pamphlet. If he was wrong it made no difference because he was going to pull the tooth anyway. *In most cases extracting the tooth will solve the problem.*

The instrument he chose was no more than six inches long. It had a T-handle at its end, which allowed a firm grip. The other end had an ugly hook curved somewhat like an awl or a blacksmith's hoof knife. Kills Many's eyes were not good up close, but when

Augustus raised the extractor to examine it more closely, the old man's eyes widened.

By now, members of the village were gathering about him, their curiosity at a high peak. Lone Grass held a page open so Augustus could quickly review the procedure. He wedged the hook in between the infected molar and the molar in front of it, just like the drawing showed. The directions recommended a quick sideward twist. Kills Many squirmed and clamped his teeth down on the instrument and Augustus' thumb. The old man stood and spoke with muffled words.

Lone Grass did not understand what he said.

"Open wider!" Augustus commanded, but the medicine man refused. Since he nervously moved about, Augustus got a neck hold on him with one arm while he struggled with his other hand to keep the extractor in place. The man had a lot of strength, but his resistance appeared to be waning.

"Sit down!" Augustus commanded. The old man sat, but still squirmed. Augustus was determined and resorted to simple strategy. He asked Lone Grass to inquire of the Chief how many horses he owned, and which was his favorite.

Kills Many stopped squirming when he heard the question, surprised that such an inquiry was delivered at that particular moment. He attempted an answer, and it was then when his jaw was relaxed that Augustus snapped the instrument sideways. When the roots tore free from the bone, Augustus cringed. The tooth popped out and fell to the ground. Kills Many had come to a full stand, and after he saw the bloody tooth lying at his feet, he sat again and put his hands back on his knees. He worked his tongue inside his mouth and spit out a gob of blood.

"Tell him to open his mouth again," said Augustus to Lone Grass.

Augustus examined the bloody hole. A procedure in the booklet said to press the tooth next to the infected one. It was not unusual for two teeth in the same area to have abscesses.

Augustus pressed the next molar. Kills Many did not wince. Carefully, Augustus examined the rest of his mouth by pressing his thumb on each of the remaining teeth. Surprisingly the man still possessed most of them, and none of them appeared to be rotting.

During the short post examination Kills Many did not stir. Augustus figured he was too scared to move, or perhaps the pressure from the abscess was finally relieved.

"Bring me my saddle bag, please," he asked Lone Grass. She complied, and Augustus retrieved a pint bottle of whiskey, half full. He unscrewed the cap and motioned for the Chief to swirl the whiskey around in his mouth and spit it out. The old man did what he asked, but before Augustus could screw the cap back on, the Chief reached for the bottle a second time. He swirled the whiskey around, but this time he swallowed it. The small crowd of onlookers laughed with approval.

Augustus backed away from the man while Lone Grass poured water over the old Chief's hands to wash away the blood. Kills Many raised up from the stump, and with a firm grip on his lance he squinted at Augustus. Augustus offered the Chief the rest of the bottle, which he accepted with a simple nod. He then spit out another gob of blood and walked away.

The next morning Augustus emerged from the tent to meet another brilliant sun on the horizon. He stretched for the longest while and breathed in the freshness of the dawn. Almost immediately, Chief Kills Many appeared and motioned for Augustus to follow him, which he did. Behind him trailed Lone Grass and Young Bear. Beyond the Chief's teepee, Augustus came to an abrupt halt. There stood a beautiful red roan horse, complete with his saddle and bridle in place. His Sharp's rifle was in the scabbard and his pistol and belt were draped over the saddle horn.

The Chief spoke for the longest time and had Lone Grass interpret for him. "Chief Kills Many says you are welcome in his camp any time. Among the Commanche you will be known as Man of Teeth, friend of Chief Kills Many."

Augustus mouth hung open. "Tell the chief I am honored."

She did so, and then, "The Chief says he will enjoy a meal with you, and afterward he will send two braves with you so that you do not get lost on the way to the Wichita Agency."

All those present enjoyed a hearty laugh. Augustus sprang into the saddle of his new horse and walked him around in a circle a few times. He dismounted, and with a wide grin he said to Lone Grass, "I'm hungry."

* * *

CHARLIE'S GOLD

Charlie swirled the water around in the pan again and thumbed the small pebbles and sand over the edge. More of the tiny gold flecks appeared in the bottom. He swirled some more and discarded more of the debris over the side of the pan with his gnarled and callused hands. In all his years of gold seeking, Charlie had never found a river creek bottom so chock full of the little golden flecks.

He had been working this area for the past six weeks. Without a doubt, this creek had been the find of his life. He grunted his satisfaction, almost wished he had someone to share his joy with. But he had learned his lesson early. Over the years, he had occasionally picked up a partner, but they all left him for one reason or another. Charlie suspected it was because lady luck just never seemed to follow him. He had been prospecting alone these past eight years or so, and really never minded it. In fact, he never considered himself alone as long as he had Old Jake, his mule. Jake was easy to talk to and never talked back. And he never seemed to mind if Charlie struck it rich or not. Old Jake was good company.

Charlie looked up at Jake. He was standing in the shade of a low oak, swishing his tail at the flies.

Charlie rested on a rock along the creek and carefully picked some more gold flecks from the bottom of his pan and placed them into his leather pouch. "Hah-hah," he laughed as he wiped a kerchief across his sweaty forehead.

Yessir, this was a strike. He searched in the bottom of the pouch and pulled out the largest of the nuggets. He held it up as if the sun would make it glitter even more. This one alone was probably worth twenty dollars.

He stared for some time at the nugget in complete satisfaction, and then suddenly his gaze was drawn beyond the nugget to the shoulder of a bluff in the north. His hand was steady as he squinted his old eyes, not sure what he had just seen. A flash of some sort.

There it was again! A brilliant but short flash. Perhaps a mirror. Somebody signaling him? Or maybe the glint off of a gun barrel!

No, not a rifle. The strange phenomenon was at least a half-mile away. That was way too far for someone to be pointing a rifle at him. Course, he had heard that rifles now a days had scopes on top of them that drew objects up close, much like his own telescope.

But if someone on the ridge was hell bent on shooting him with such a long-range gun, he would already be dead.

No. This was something different. His mind whirled, plagued him with random thoughts of what was going on. But, in order not to arouse suspicion, just in case it was somebody, Charlie acted as natural as he could. He dare not even think about reaching for the Winchester on the bank. No sense in giving himself away.

He crawled up the bank from the water and stood on the pathway he had worn down in the past six weeks, a narrow stretch that paralleled the shoreline and led back to where his tent was tucked securely underneath an overhanging ledge. That was good protection, not only from the wind and rain, but also, from anyone approaching from the north. That's the only way anyone could enter this boxed-in gulch. From the south, no more than a few hundred yards, the creek, flowing like an underground river, appeared magically from under a huge rock face. Basically, the south end of this narrow canyon offered Charlie protection from that direction. The cliffs jutted almost straight upwards in a jagged fashion. There was no way anyone could come down those cliffs unless one had three hundred feet of rope.

The only way out of this canyon was a day's walk to the north where the river opened to the flat plains. The nearest town, Wolf Flats, was 120 miles back east, at least a five-day walk for Charlie and his mule. That's where he had originally come from.

This was a remote area, just the kind of pickings Charlie liked.

But today was a cause for concern. Charlie now had a fair notion who was up on the bluff. On the way in, six weeks back, he had run across three cowboys, or so they said they were. But Charlie knew they weren't cowboys. Their hands were too smooth, and their horses weren't muscled cow ponies, but nags. And only one of the three had a lariat on his saddle. No cowboy would travel without a rope.

They said they were looking for Wolf Flats, lost they said. But Charlie knew better. Anyone coming across the flats had to know Wolf Flats was at the far side of the plain. Otherwise no one crossed those flats. And there was only one water hole along the way. By horseback, a good rider could make the trek in two days easy, that is, if he traveled by night when it was cooler. These boys hadn't even asked for a drink from Charlie, so they had water in their canteens. And they knew where they were headed.

Charlie had been cautious when he first met them, and also very observant. One had to be when one traveled alone.

"Seen your tracks," one of the young men had remarked.

"Damn, you fellers are a couple real trackers," Charlie remembered he had answered. They nodded, seemed to appreciate his humor. Crossing the flats for a few days without wind left a sure trail. Any fool could follow tracks like that, even a blind fool. Charlie had trekked across the desert from Wolf Flats, and the three young fellows knew it. And they must have surmised, it seemed to Charlie, that he was on his way out prospecting, not coming back in. They had inquired about the direction of Wolf Flats, and when Charlie pointed to the east, they just nodded and headed off in that direction.

Charlie had kept an eye on them, and after about three miles, the trio headed off to the north. So Charlie knew they weren't headed for Wolf Flats. He thought that strange at the time, but in the past six weeks, he hadn't given it any further thought. He figured they might have been drifters, headed nowhere in particular.

But now he was once again concerned. His first guess was it was these three young fellows up on the bluff who were keeping an eye on him. Out here in the middle of nowhere, there would be only one reason why. Charlie wiped his forehead, not sure the sweat was from the heat or from worry. But he couldn't quit panning now. It was afternoon, and if he suddenly walked back to the tent, which was out of the ordinary for him, they might become suspicious.

Charlie didn't have any alternative. He waded back into the creek, dipped his pan in the bottom and drew up some gravel. He worked the creek for another two hours, but every now and then he glanced in the direction of the bluff. Surprisingly, he had not seen any more activity, and now, on occasion, he began to scan the cliff tops all around him.

Another hour passed without seeing any sign of them.

Charlie began to worry. It wasn't so much of a problem here at the end of the canyon. Charlie had strategically placed his tent under a protruding ledge precisely for that reason. Anyone coming towards camp would arouse Old Jake, his mule, who could hear a frog fart from a mile away. Usually his ears perked up with any unusual sound, and then he would start braying, more in the form of a light wheeze, since Old Jake, in mule years was older then Charlie.

Charlie's eyes were good for an old man, and his aim was still pretty good. Of course, the three boys up on the rise—if indeed it was the three—didn't know that. That gave Charlie some comfort, knowing he could pick off the head of a wheat stalk at 100 yards, giving the wind was still.

"Damn," Charlie said again as he crawled up the bank. He grabbed his Winchester and began making his way along the path toward his tent. It was already sundown, normal quitting time for him. This gulch was so deep, that sundown came early and sunup came late. That made his day kind of short, which he really didn't mind. In the past few years, a lot of sleep each night seemed to give him more and more comfort. He wondered how he would sleep to-night.

The trek to the camp was only a few minutes, but he didn't look back, didn't dare for fear he would give himself away. There was no need to alert the fellow, or fellows, who were up on the bluff. That set Charlie to wondering how long he had been under observation. That was very inconsiderate and an invasion of his privacy. If whoever was up there had been observing him for the past six weeks, he must also have known Charlie had panned a goodly amount of glitter out of this creek.

Yet, it didn't seem likely that someone would sit up on a bank for six weeks waiting for a prospector to gather up his gold. One had to eat. One had to drink.

Then, of course, if there were three of them, one could always go back for vittles and drink. Two could stay, one could go back, or one could stay and two could go back.

The more Charlie thought, the more worried he became. He might be able to fight off three, but then, they could have gone back for reinforcements. By the time Charlie reached his tent, he had conjured up in his mind a whole passel of cowboys. Highwaymen, that is.

He leaned his Winchester against a stump outside his tent, a sign that he wasn't on to the would-be robbers. Once inside the tent he hunted up his telescope.

"Two can play this game," he said as he settled in a shadowed corner of the tent, a point from where he could observe the ridge and yet not be observed. He peered through the telescope in the direction of the high ridge where he had first seen signs of the intruder.

For a few minutes he saw nothing and figured it might be senseless to watch forever, but then a figure was suddenly there. The man was hatless, at least now. Then another head popped up next to him, and then a third!

There was no doubt it was the same three that had approached him several weeks back. The third man had bright red hair, and now, with the sun up on the rise, the man's hair looked like it was on fire. Yes, the red haired man was one of the three. At least Charlie now was relatively sure there were only three. And one of them was looking back at him through a telescope. The flash he had seen earlier must have been a glint off the eyeglass. Charlie was certain they couldn't see him looking up at them through a similar eyepiece. They had remained a long ways away, and evidently were smart enough to keep their distance. From where Charlie sat he had a very good view of the creek bed approach, and would have no trouble keeping some would-be intruders at bay.

Charlie's confidence increased a bit. He put the telescope away, went outside and built a fire. Soon he had coffee boiling and brought out some jerky from a deer he had shot sometime back. His beans had been long gone, and there were very few roots down here in this gulch, so he was pretty much restricted to deer meat. All the while he was outside, he was feeling fairly comfortable, but when night came, a course of the jitters hit him. He did not sleep much during the night, though he well could have, since Old Jake, his mule, had never failed him before. If the three were dumb enough to try and surprise him in the night, it would not have been easy for them. The nearly full moon made it fairly easy to see, especially for Charlie, since his tent was completely shadowed by the overhanging ledge above. Though brush, small olive trees and an occasional wild oak dotted the creek sides, Charlie still had a clear view of the area. Even the flow of the water in the creek was slow enough that it did not give off a gurgle, no rushing sounds of any sort.

Charlie had reconciled himself to the fact that he would have to simply go about his business of panning gold. For the next three days that's exactly what he did. But he was always on the alert, occasionally checking the ridge where he had first seen the men. They had made an appearance every day, sometimes for as much as ten minutes at a spell. And then sometimes as much as a half-day might pass before he would catch another glimpse of them. But they were there, waiting, Charlie was sure, for the day he would pack up and head out of the gulch. Somewhere along the way they would hold him up, maybe even drygulch him. It amused Charlie, that perhaps that was where the word *drygulch* came from. And then, of course, it wasn't amusing, because he might be the one that was *drygulched!*

Two more days passed and gave Charlie a lot of time to think. He had acquired quite a bit of gold, but the question was how was he going to get himself and the gold past these three highwaymen? The creek was still producing glitter, but not at the rate like when he had first started panning. For the most part, Charlie was satisfied that he had already procured a large share of what gold this creek was going to produce. He had covered over three hundred yards of the creek bottom, he figured. Most of the nuggets had showed up right here, near the south end of the canyon.

It was time to move out, but he couldn't do that without a battle plan. That night one came to him in a dream so real, that he found himself suddenly awake and unable to go back to sleep. At first light, he was up and immediately began formulating his preparation to strike camp. By mid morning, Charlie had packed his pick and shovel, along with the tent and most everything else he had arrived with. If a person was to leave a gold digging sight, he was leaving for one of two reasons; either he didn't find anything, or he had enough gold to go into town and celebrate.

Obviously the three up on the cliff had seen him stuff nuggets into his leather pouch. Course, they would have no exact notion of how much he had panned or how many actual dollars he had on him. But anyone that left a gold digging sight either left with gold or without it. Charlie was leaving with gold, and he was sure the would-be robbers up above knew it.

When Charlie draped his final wares on the mule, a bag with pots and pans in it, he casually glanced across the top of the pack-saddle. The boys were there. As he headed down the path, he maintained a casual lookout. In short time the figure that had been there disappeared. It didn't take Charlie long to reach the narrows, the place directly beneath where the three were stationed. He did not bother to look up, or give any indication he knew they were in the vicinity. That was part of the battle plan—to make it appear they had the element of surprise. The Winchester was strapped on the back of Old Jake, the stock sticking up out of a scabbard, it too in plain sight and part of the plan. After all, he needed some sort of deterrent.

Charlie was fairly certain the three would strike near the end of the canyon where it opened to the plains. There was plenty brush, an easy place to hide and create an ambush.

A total ambush was something Charlie wasn't counting on. If they drygulched him on the spot, all of his efforts this morning would have gone for naught. If they did decide to shoot him, he hoped their aim would be good, and that they would shoot him through the heart. His worst fear was he might be gut shot and left to die over the next two or three days. That would be mighty painful.

But Charlie was looking on the positive side of things. The least he could expect was to be kicked around a bit. That had happened to him on more than one occasion during his lifetime. But getting kicked around *just a bit* really never killed anybody.

Charlie and Jake plugged along, as if nothing in the world concerned them. Charlie even caught himself whistling once in awhile. And even though he stopped, it seemed that a few minutes later he would once again start up whistling.

The sun was coming high over the walls of the canyon now, and Charlie, as unobtrusively as possible, managed a periodic glance upwards, thinking he might catch a glimpse of the three men. But they had made themselves scarce for the moment.

Shortly past noon he had not seen a thing. It caused him to wonder whether he had judged the boys wrongly. Perhaps they were just having a gander at him for the fun of it. No, they had been there better than a week. They weren't hanging around, thinking Old Charlie was going to hang himself from a low tree branch and leave them the gold without a fight.

No, sir. Charlie had a battle plan. He had been rehearsing it in his mind since he left, and perhaps that's why he had unconsciously found himself whistling when he shouldn't be. The plan would go something like this. Once they stopped him, he would wield off a few remarks how the pickings had not been so good. They in turn would tell him they had been watching him for sometime and knew he had gold on him. He would then make up some excuse that his whole life had been dedicated to prospecting without ever hitting it big, and that he...

"Hold it right there, mister," he suddenly heard. Charlie stopped dead in his tracks, and then slowly turned and saw the man. He definitely was one of the three men Charlie had seen earlier, and he was standing no more than twenty yards away. But the holdup had been struck a little earlier than he figured, and how anyone had gotten this close to him without Old Jake perking up his ears was a sudden mystery. Charlie gave his mule a contemptuous look.

He made a feeble reach for his Winchester, knowing he had to grant some sort of resistance.

"Don't even try it, old timer," came another voice from somewhere off to the left. Then ahead of him was the third man, and all three had their pistols drawn.

"We been watching you for some time, old man. You can make it easy if you just hand over the gold real gentle like. Then we'll be on our way and you'll be on yours."

The boy doing all the talking so far was the red-haired youngster. None of the boys was even twenty years old, Charlie calculated. He started putting his battle plan into effect. "Hell, boys, you picked the wrong day to rob Old Charlie. Was a time, back in sixty-three when I was up Montana way. In them days pickings was pretty decent. Why I remember one time, just outside Virginia City, I was..."

"Shut up, old man, and hand over the gold," said the young fellow in front of him. "We know you got plenty."

"Just hand it over and there won't be no trouble," said the red-haired boy.

"Like I was saying," Charlie continued, "if you had hit me in Virginia City, I would have..."

Before Charlie could finish, a backhand caught him across the face and reeled him flat to the ground.

Charlie felt a drip of blood on his lip and swiped it away. "Hell, I been knocked down before by a lot bigger fellers than you." The young man suddenly swung a foot into Charlie's midsection, and Charlie belted out a terrible grunt.

"Frank, dammit!" said one of the other men. "No need to beat him up. Let's just get the gold and get out of here."

To Charlie, those were sweet words of comfort. The three were all on the scene now. The young man, who had been referred to as *Frank*, was now searching Charlie's clothing, running his hands all over, inside his vest, around his waist. "He ain't got no belt on him."

The young man twisted his face and spit out, "Take off your clothes."

Charlie stared at the man.

"Take em off. Strip down!"

Charlie pulled off his jacket, followed by his vest, shirt and pants. As he removed the articles of clothing, the three searched every piece, looking for the pouch.

Charlie stood silently, clad only in his longjohns and boots. With no gold visible, the three turned to the pack mule. They stripped off the bag of pots and pans, then another bag with drygoods and jerky, more clothing, then the tent. They rummaged through everything, even ejected the shells out of the Winchester, thinking he might have stuffed nuggets into the magazine. They emptied some mementos from a leather bag, which also contained a small caliber pistol. After everything was taken out and gone through, they still did not find any gold.

The red-haired fellow took command again. "Take off your boots, old man," he demanded.

"Shucks, ain't nothing in my..."

The man struck another blow to Charlie, knocking him to the ground. Immediately, the other two tugged fiercely at Charlie's boots. But Charlie, just to try their patience, curled up his toes holding the boots on. Finally, with a heavy sigh, Charlie relaxed his toes and the boots came off, and out of each boot fell a small leather pouch.

The man with the fiery red hair grinned. "What'd I tell you boys. I knowed all along he made a find."

Frank, the youngest of the three, and the one who had first knocked Charlie to the ground, opened both of the pouches and poured out the nuggets. Two of the boys seemed happy with the find, but the redhead wasn't. "Hell, this ain't barely a hundred dollars, he said." Old man, we seen you take more than this out of that creek. Where's the rest?

"Maybe he left it back at camp," one of the others offered.

"A man don't dig for gold and then leave without it," the red head retorted.

"I swear," said Charlie, his face loading with more fear all the time. "The pickings warn't what I expected. There ain't no one here more disappointed than I am."

The red-head now turned ugly, and kicked at Charlie, more out of disgust, since the blow just barely brushed Charlie's leg.

The other two men were now tearing through everything that was on the packsaddle. They ripped the seams of the tent apart, shredded the clothing, cut apart every cloth and leather bag.

"There ain't nothing here, Frank," said one of the men.

The red-haired fellow glared at the mule, then at Charlie. Charlie edged backward, thinking another boot was going to be coming at him.

Then, the red-haired fellow stomped over to the mule and unleashed the latigo and let the packsaddle drop to the ground. He flipped over the saddle, and there, underneath, he saw the fresh stitching. His fingers shook with nervousness as he pulled a knife from his pocket. In seconds he sliced through the stitches. Charlie couldn't have made a glummer face.

"Eee-hah!" hollered the redhead as he ripped the leather seam apart. The gold nuggets dropped to the ground in a small pile.

The sudden discovery made its impact. The three had the most greedy and smug looking faces Charlie had ever seen. "Thought you could pull a fast one on us, eh, old timer?"

The three scooped up the nuggets and added them to the two leather pouches they had taken from Charlie.

"Boys," said Charlie with a saddened and dejected face. "I worked that creek for nigh on to two months. You got to leave me some of it."

But the three weren't listening. "Must be three or four hundred dollars here!" said one of them.

"We done hit it big!" said another.

One of the men walked off and came back with their three horses.

"You ain't leaving me nothing?" asked Charlie.

"We're leaving you with your life, old man. You're lucky we didn't kill you."

The red-haired man then picked up Charlie's Winchester and the old pistol, and heaved both into the creek. "And so's you don't starve to death, you got your guns too. We'll be long gone before you retrieve them. And don't get any dumb ideas about trying to catch up to us."

Charlie raised himself off the ground. "Don't think you got to worry about that, son. Old Jake and I couldn't outrun a dead rattlesnake."

The three boys laughed with the comment. "At least he's got a sense of humor," said one of them. With that, the three swung into their saddles, whirled their horses around and trotted off down the canyon.

The first thing Charlie did after the men were out of sight, was wade into the water where his Winchester and pistol had been thrown. The water was clear, and the two weapons were easy to spot. They would both fire once they dried out. Charlie was remotely surprised they left his weapons for him. Weapons or not, he might have gotten hungry, but he could have made it back to Wolf Flats without them.

Charlie returned to where he had been robbed, put his clothes and boots on, then lashed the pack saddle to Jake, and in spite of fact that everything had been either shredded or ripped apart, he carefully packed it all on.

Charlie found his hat, put it in place and glanced in the direction where the three highwaymen had disappeared. They were not to be seen, and Charlie was more than certain he would never see them again.

"Yessir," said Charlie to Old Jake. "That was one hell of a battle plan." He grabbed Jake by the lead rope, turned and headed back up the canyon, back to where his camp was. The three boys had got away with a little over four hundred dollars in gold, Charlie figured. But back at his camp sight, he had the rest of his gold cached in two small leather parfleches.

Over four thousand dollars he had calculated, and all it had cost him was four hundred dollars in bait. He also got a split lip and a kick in the gut, but on more than one occasion he had got much worse than that for cheating at cards. So this was a pretty good trade-off.

"Yessir," he said to Old Jake again as he trudged along the creek. "That was one hell of a battle plan."

* * *

THE BANK JOB

Charles Howen's real name was Charles Hayden. He knew cattle and horses, and he had spent the better part of ten years bringing herds up from Texas. Before the war, he drove cattle to Chicago, and right after the war he had delivered herds to Sedalia, Missouri. As the railroads pushed westward, so did the cattle pens, and in the successive years, he had brought herds to Kansas City, Lawrence, Abilene and Ellsworth. The sad part was none of these herds were his. In the early days he was just a cowpuncher, but had worked up to the position of foreman. That was a little better pay, but it was still hard work. Charles Hayden was now past thirty and did not relish the thought of spending the rest of his life driving cattle for someone else.

He didn't know much else other than cattle and horses, and he had no interest in farming or working in a town mercantile store. He didn't like peddling, so sales was out. In fact he did not like much of anything except the open range. But he was tired of working for somebody else, and he wasn't getting rich.

In recent years, the Western Cattle Trail had opened up, and now herds were being driven up from Texas to Ogalalla. Since Ogallala was now a new market, cattle coming in meant a lot of dollars were on hand, cash to pay for prime beef. Charles knew the bank in Ogalala was busting at the seams with money. How much, he didn't know for sure, but it was a lot.

So Charles Hayden had decided, some time back, to rob it.

He wasn't going to just walk in and hold it up like the James Gang. He considered himself a bit more sophisticated than those boys. He intended to reconnoiter this bank, and reconnoiter it well.

It was a sunny, July morning when Charles Hayden walked through the front door of the Ogallala Bank for the first time.

"Yessir, Mr. Howen," said the teller from behind the counter. "We can sure take care of that for you." He accepted the five hundred dollars in bills, wrote out a receipt in the name of *Charles Howen* and handed it back to the tall man. "If you'll sign here," the teller asked.

The tall man signed the paperwork.

"From Texas, you say, Mr. Howen?" the teller asked.

"That's right," the tall man answered. "Just outside of Fort Worth.

"What might be your business here, if you don't mind my asking?" He was a little fellow. He lifted the frame of his glasses off his nose as if to relieve an irritation of some sort, and waited for a response.

"Horses," said the tall man. "Interested in purchasing some horses."

"Well, now," said the teller. "Perhaps you'd like to talk to Mr. Bancroft, the president of our bank. He's got a spread outside of town and raises horses. And sells them, too," he quickly added.

Charles Hayden already knew that, and he also expected the bespectacled man to make such an offer.

"Well, that's some coincidence," said the Texan. "I'd sure appreciate a few minutes with him."

"Yessir, if you'll wait right here, I'll inform him." The man skirted around the counter and disappeared through a back door. While he was gone, Charles Hayden leaned on the counter and nonchalantly looked around the bank. The teller, it appeared, was the only employee. A writing stand was the only piece of furniture on the west wall directly beneath a window. This window and two others, one on each side of the front door, were lined with thin bars.

A counter ran the length of the room, and behind it on the back wall were pigeonhole receptacles lining each side of a huge vault door, which was closed. There didn't appear to be another exit to the outside from this room, at least not from his vantagepoint. But there was a hallway off to the right of the door where the teller had disappeared. He wondered where that led to.

The door to the president's office opened and the teller came out, followed by Mr. Bancroft, a rather short, stout man with thick white hair and bushy white eyebrows. The teller introduced the two, and in moments Charles was invited into the president's office. First off, Mr. Bancroft thanked the Texan for making the deposit in his bank, and assured him it was as safe as money could be. Charles Hayden took a chair and immediately indicated his interest in acquiring some horses of good stock, and said he was willing to pay top price for good quality.

Mr. Bancroft's grin widened as he opened a box of cigars and offered one to the Texan. Blue smoke soon filled the room while the two engaged in lengthy horse talk. They discussed Morgans and quarter horses and Arabians. They discussed conformation and other qualities of horse breeds, and talked about the length of the stride of a Tennessee Walker. Both were well informed about horses and horse breeding.

While they talked, the Texan, very much at ease, was attentive to his surroundings. When the president opened a drawer, he moved a .38 caliber nickel-plated Colt to the side as he searched for registered papers on his horses. When Mr. Bancroft leaned over the desk, the Texan spotted the small .32 Harrington & Richardson revolver tucked in a shoulder holster under his coat.

There was no exit from this room, except the one he came through. Two windows gave a view to the back alley, but both were laden with heavy bars. Under a long table behind his desk was a smaller safe, dark green. It probably weighed at least five hundred pounds, Hayden guessed, and it more than likely had some cash in it, perhaps even jewelry. Quite often bankers had such safes, which were accessible at any minute of the day, unlike the huge vault in the lobby which had a time lock on it.

"You say you just delivered some cattle to Ellsworth?" the banker inquired in-between puffs.

"Yessir," answered the Texan confidently. "My partner, Mr. Hale, should be arriving within the next few days. I'm guessing he must have the cattle sold already." There was no partner named Mr. Hale. Charles expected the man to ask what brand he was driving, and though he had a legitimate brand in mind, to his surprise, Mr. Bancroft didn't inquire.

The banker squinted his eyes. "Big herd was it you delivered?"

"Oh, I don't know if you consider 3500 head big or not," said the Texan as he leaned back in his chair and blew out a stream of smoke. He crossed a leg, and when he did so, his long coat draped downward exposing the .45 Colt at his side. The banker saw the revolver, but thought nothing of it. Men carried revolvers all the time. Especially cattlemen. Of course, Charles Hayden wanted him to see the revolver. It was nickel plated, like the banker's .38, and it was fairly new resting inside a slick, black holster.

In fact, Charles Hayden wanted the man to examine him from head to toe. He was wearing a nice blue suit, a long tan slicker of excellent quality, and dressed with a fine, white shirt and string tie, something he rarely wore. His boots were made of the best leather and not at all worn out like the boots of a cowboy fresh off of a thousand mile cattle drive.

Charles Hayden had spent a lot of money on himself, and the five hundred dollars he had deposited in the bank was all the cash he had. Everything about him, he hoped, looked very legitimate. Now, sitting in the banker's office, contemplating a robbery, he was even surprised how calm he was. He was even enjoying himself. The role seemed so natural to him.

The banker was calculating in his head. He knew thirty five hundred head of cattle would bring about twelve dollars apiece in today's market. He thought he was looking at a rancher who had a large sum of money on hand, or at least had access to a large sum of money. Money always interested Mr. Bancroft.

The banker leaned forward. "You said you were looking to purchase some horses?"

"Yes," answered the Texan.

The banker held out his hands somewhat confused. "But your partner...is arriving in a few days or so, you said." There was a big pause. "To simply buy a few horses?"

The Texan smiled, "We're going to need horses down the rode apiece. A Texan ain't a Texan without horses, you know. Actually, my partner and I are more interested in real estate, maybe make some investments along that line. With the cattle coming up this way now, I'm guessing the town of Ogallala's gonna do some fast growing. "

Mr. Bancroft's eyes lit up even more, something, which did not at all escape note by Charles Hayden. Charles knew the banker held a lot of property, something he had researched a long time ago. The more he knew about Mr. Bancroft, the better. After all, he was planning on robbing the man.

Another fifteen minutes passed during which time the two discussed real estate holdings available in the town. Mr. Bancroft held the deeds to several pieces of land he personally owned, and the deeds, naturally, were in the green safe behind him. When he worked the combination, Hayden noticed he only turned the dial once to the right. Mr. Bancroft was a practical man, something the Texan liked. More than likely he opened that safe several times a day. It may have had three numbers on it, but he obviously had dialed in the first few digits earlier. Now, he had simply moved the combination to the last number. And while the banker was sorting through the deeds over the top of his desk, Hayden happened to notice that the pointer on the combination dial was set on the number *five*.

That was a valuable bit of information to acquire. Before he left the room, he also learned that the time lock on the vault was set for 9:20 sharp each morning, exactly 35 minutes after the bank opened its doors. And inside that vault was enough cash to handle the immediate needs of any drovers bringing their cattle this way. Charles Hayden knew three herds were already on the Western Cattle Trail bound for Ogallala.

On the way out of the President's office, the Texan graciously accepted a handful of fine cigars, just like the one he had smoked earlier. The two talked for a few more minutes in the doorway, and while they did, the Texan made sure he had placed himself strategically so he could view the hallway. Another door led somewhere, and while he was wondering where to, it opened, and in came a young lady who was introduced to the Texan as Mr. Bancroft's daughter. She was a pretty thing with a little turned up nose, and her black hair stood out against the pink dress trimmed in lace. Mr. Bancroft announced her as "My daughter, Constance." The Texan hoped he had made an impression on the banker. Perhaps too much of an impression, for it seemed the man made a point of introducing her as *a young lady of culture who had caught the eye of many a young man.*

Had caught, the Texan thought to himself. That implied she was still on the loose. The Texan took off his hat and bowed, all the time thinking Mr. Bancroft was making a small effort at being a matchmaker. More importantly, what he learned from the short conversation, was that the door she had come through led to the Bancroft's living quarters. Charles thought it strange that a banker would live next door to his own bank. It wasn't unusual for merchants to have their homes in the back of their stores or above them, but the few bankers that Charles knew owned rather prominent homes apart from their place of business.

Since Mr. Bancroft lived next door, that meant besides the front door to the bank, this doorway to his living quarters was the only other exit. More than likely there were both front and rear entrances in the living quarters.

Miss Bancroft was on her way out the front of the bank, so Charles politely opened the swinging door, which separated the front lobby from the back counter. As he did so he could not help but notice the sawed off shotgun underneath the cage where the teller worked.

Also, the vault was now open, which meant the time was after 9:20.

Charles Hayden escorted the young lady past a few people out the door, once again took off his hat and bid her good day. He watched her walk down the boardwalk, mildly intrigued by the tiny steps she took. She was a most polite lady, even comfortable to be with. At least to talk to. After she disappeared into one of the shops, Charles walked in the opposite direction to the livery.

No one was around when he entered. He walked past several stalls until he came to his horse, a big, stout sorrel, sixteen hands high. He was a well-muscled horse and had the stamina of a long rider. On this sorrel, Charles could ride all day and put on eighty miles. After a short four-hour rest and some gamma grass, this horse was ready to do another eighty.

With a big, fast horse like this, he could make the Dakota Territory within a couple days. In another hard week of riding he could reach Montana.

Since nobody was around to tend to his horse, Charles drew up a can of oats. While his horse was eating, he threw on his fancy saddle, which had cost him more than the horse.

To look like a rich cattle rancher, he had to dress the part. And now, to make it look like he was interested in real estate, he had to make the rounds of the town. He would make a few inquiries, look over some lots, and maybe check out the piece of grass north of town, which Mr. Bancroft had mentioned.

He led his horse out of the stable, climbed into the saddle and headed down the middle of Main Street.

As he ambled along, he was thinking what a nice, sunny day it was. At the corner he glanced toward the store where he had seen Miss Constance disappear no more than a half-hour ago. She was just coming out.

"Ma'am," Charles Hayden said as he touched the brim of his hat. She nodded back. He did like her, even though their meeting had been brief. There was a certain charm about her, the way she smiled, the way she bobbed her head when she spoke.

It was a shame he had to rob her father's bank, but he had come to Ogallala on bank robbing business. Every dollar he owned was tied up in his horse and gear, in his clothes and boots and new revolver and holster, and in the new Winchester in the scabbard on his saddle. And of course several years of savings in the amount of five hundred dollars, which was now in the Ogallala Bank. That five hundred was just seed money, a teaser, so to speak.

Charles Hayden had been driving cattle for years, and in all those years he hadn't accumulated much more than a thousand dollars. That was all the more reason to rob a bank.

"Dang, she sure is a pretty thing," he said to himself again. Curiously, he turned in his saddle to look back where she had been standing on the boardwalk. She was still there looking back at him, but then quickly walked on toward the bank.

Charles Hayden was both amused and flattered. Was she interested in him? He shrugged off the notion and straightened up in his saddle.

It was too early for a visit to a saloon, so he headed for the blacksmith's shop. The right front shoe of his horse needed some attention, and while the blacksmith was checking his horse's foot, a middle-aged man came over to pick up his mule. The man walked with a slouch, spoke with a heavy southern accent and wasn't dressed very well. He was carrying a sidearm, but it was an old Navy Colt, a cap and ball model, and even had a spot of rust on the hammer, Charles noticed. What impressed Charles most, was the man was wearing a badge.

"He's the deputy," said the blacksmith after the man left. He drove a fresh nail into the shoe on Charles' horse, bent it over and clipped it, then examined the rest of the feet.

"This fellow's in good shape," said the blacksmith. "Good

feet, long muscled legs. I'll bet he's got a lot of endurance."

Charles smiled to himself. The blacksmith couldn't have been more accurate in his assessment of the animal.

"Now, take Alvin's mule," he said as he motioned in the direction where the Deputy had disappeared. That mule couldn't do ten miles before his feet give out. Too old, anyway, to be good for much of anything."

That was useful information, Charles was thinking. He could outrun a mule any day, and a mule with bad feet was better yet.

"Does the Sheriff ride a mule, too." Charles asked jokingly.

"No," the blacksmith answered with a smile as he rolled a stubby burned out cigar from one side of his mouth to another. "He's got a good horse, but he's over in Scotts Bluff delivering a prisoner or picking one up, I don't remember which. That'll be fifty cents."

Charles paid him and offered him a cigar. "Here, looks like you're about due for another one."

The blacksmith examined the cigar. "You must have got that from Harold."

"Harold?"

"Harold at the bank. He's the only one in town who smokes that kind of cigar. I've heard he imports them." He lit up the cigar, puffed on it and nodded as he examined it again. "You're new around here, ain't you?"

"Yeah," answered Charles. "You know Harold pretty well?"

"Who don't? He's been here a long time and he's done good, and he seems to treat people right. Course, he lives like most of the rest of us, right next door to his bank." He puffed on the cigar, obviously admiring the taste of it. "Got a good looking daughter, too." He winked at Charles when he spoke. "She's caught the attention of a lot of young fellows, but those that approached her been turned down regular."

"Why's that?" asked Charles.

The blacksmith thought a moment. "Oh, I suppose cause she's had a bit of schooling. You know, one of them colleges back east. She ain't uppity or nothing like that. It's just that the boys around here ain't quite to her liking, if you know what I mean."

The man eyed a buggy near by. "I suppose I better get to fixing that wheel, or Elmer ain't going to get home tonight."

Hayden thanked the man for his time, climbed on his horse and rode back to the livery through the back alley. As he passed the rear of the bank, he took note of the back door to Mr. Bancroft's living quarters.

He put his horse back in the stable, then returned to the hotel where he located a chair near a corner window overlooking the street and the bank. By late afternoon, he had drunk almost a pot of coffee, but not once had young Miss Constance appeared on the street.

Later in the evening he had supper at a nearby restaurant. He was in bed early, and up early the next morning. It was a Sunday, and practically no one was on the street. After breakfast in the hotel, he went to the livery, saddled up and rode out of town. The spread Mr. Bancroft had mentioned was about six miles northeast, he remembered. He would know it by a broken down corral, the only structure in the area.

It was another sunny morning and very pleasant, and inside of an hour, he found the corral. He spent another hour riding the rolling hills until he located the creek, which was the western border. From that point the property ran north about two miles, then east to the road that led back to Ogallala. The grass was good. Charles estimated the size of the spread would handle about eight hundred head of cattle.

Back on the Ogallala road he mentally began calculating the cost of a small herd. In Texas he could buy cattle for around four dollars a head. He could gather up longhorns on the loose for no price at all. He had to pay a crew, and there was grub and a chuck wagon, horses, a wrangler, other expenses. He was looking at a three thousand dollar investment, minimum.

By the time he reached Ogallala, he realized he once again was working on a dream. Many times before he had calculated a similar scenario. Three thousand was a lot of money, virtually impossible for him to raise, and besides, he had to buy the spread first. That would be another outlay of money. All the more reason to rob a bank.

In any case, the ride served the purpose of giving him a good lay of the land that he planned to use as his escape route.

A few buggies were now coming back out of Ogallala, churchgoers, he was sure, returning to their farms or ranches. Back on Main Street, he headed for the livery.

"Mr. Howen," he heard someone call. He was so preoccupied with his thoughts, that he had not seen Mr. Bancroft escorting his daughter. Evidently, the two had just attended church, since they were dressed in their Sunday best.

Hayden stopped his horse, got off and removed his hat. "Morning," he offered.

"I see you've been out riding, Mr. Howen."

"Yessir, I decided to take a look at that piece of range you mentioned.

"It's fine grass, Mr. Howen. I can make you a deal you can't turn down. Maybe even throw in a horse or two."

Charles nodded. "I'm sure you could."

"Would you care to join us for an evening meal? We could talk it over."

Charles Hayden didn't want to accept the offer, but he had said he was interested in acquiring some property, so, really, how could he turn him down? Miss Constance had not said a word, simply held fast to her father's arm. Her constant smile was almost mesmerizing.

"Yessir, I'd appreciate that very much."

That evening, Charles Hayden called at the Bancroft residence. Once again, Mr. Bancroft and his daughter, Constance, greeted him. When he thought back, he realized that there had been no mention about Mrs. Bancroft. During the course of the evening, he learned she had died while giving birth to Constance, and Mr. Bancroft had never remarried.

It was a splendid meal of pork chops, potatoes, onions, home made biscuits and bread pudding for dessert. Though the Bancrofts had a maid, Hayden noticed that Miss Constance spent a lot of her time in the kitchen helping with the preparation.

It was a comfortable evening in one respect; the meal was very good, and he very much enjoyed the company of the young lady. She was most polite and well schooled like the blacksmith had said. In fact, when a local political issue became a part of the conversation, she did not agree with her father on several points, but their disagreements were cordial, though without resolution.

Later in the evening after the maid was dismissed, Mr. Bancroft discussed the availability of various pieces of property in and around the town of Ogallala. He expounded at length on the quality of the grassland, which Charles had inspected that day, although he did not mention a price.

The man occasionally presented a few questions, and Charles gave his observations. His answers were as positive as he could make them, and for the most part, they were dreams he actually had, although he had no way to pay for them. It wasn't exactly lying, he kept reminding himself as the evening moved on. As comfortable as the two had made it for him, things still weren't sitting well with him. The situation had become too personal. It had been a long time since he had been invited to a meal in someone's home. The last time he had had this kind of attention was during the few years he spent with his aunt and uncle who had raised him. But that was years ago, and they were long dead.

Still, this was a business deal. Did Mr. Bancroft treat all his clients in this manner? Was this simply his method of doing business? The blacksmith had said Mr. Bancroft treated his customers fairly.

"It's getting late," Charles finally said. It wasn't that late, but he didn't feel comfortable with his situation any longer. He had a strong urge to return to the hotel, maybe have a brandy or two.

Mr. Bancroft didn't object, and said he would expect Charles to pay him a visit at the bank in the morning. The man could not have been more correct, Charles was thinking. He thanked them for the meal and left.

That night Charles Hayden sat in his bedroom and mulled over the activities of the day. The one thing he forced himself to do was separate his personal relationship with the Bancrofts from his eventual goal, which was to rob the bank. He rehearsed over and over in his mind how he would go about it. He now knew the exit of the bank hallway lead directly through the Bancroft's living room. The door was a heavy one, but with a simple lock. It didn't have to be a steel door, since the vault was on a time lock, and the safe in the back room would require extraordinary measures to haul it away. For all practical purposes, the bank could only be robbed when the vault was open.

It was taking shape. He would enter the front, have his horse out back. Once he had the money from the vault, he would exit through the Bancroft's home to the alley. He decided not to consider robbing the safe in Mr. Bancroft's office. With a little luck, he could get the vault money and exit through the back alley without even alerting Mr. Bancroft. With the fast horse he was riding, he wouldn't need much of a lead. It made no difference that people had seen his face, because once he was out of Ogallala, he never planned on coming back. And once he reached Dakota Territory he was out of Nebraska's jurisdiction.

The next morning he rose with the sun, lucky if he had four hours sleep. For the next few hours he simply stared out the window of his second story room onto the street below. The bank was straight across, and he could see the back corral of the livery. That's where he would tie up his horse. He had seen other men tie their horses there while they did business at various shops along that north street. It was no more than fifty yards from the back door of the Bancroft residence to the corral.

It was a perfect set up. Mr. Bancroft would be expecting him this morning and would more than likely inform his teller that he would be arriving. Charles would wait across the street at the hotel until he was sure no one was in the bank. At that time he would enter, check for any other possible people, then lock the front door. He shouldn't have any trouble overpowering the teller. He knew where the man kept the shotgun, and he would wait for a strategic moment when the man was far enough away from the weapon to make his move.

Once he had the vault money, and, assuming the vault had a ventilating system, he would lock the teller inside. He would lay his gun barrel across the teller's head only as a last resort. He didn't like the idea, but if necessary he would do it. Under no circumstances would he kill anyone. He never had before, never even came close. He had never robbed anyone either, but for sure he would not kill anybody.

His escape route would be through the Bancroft's residence. If the door were locked, he would shoot the lock off.

He felt he was prepared for everything. He had reworked the plan over and over in his head so often, it was like clockwork. He knew he could pull it off.

Any second thoughts he had about Miss Constance, he cast aside. She was a charming person, perhaps someone he could even become interested in, but he had come too far, invested a lot of time and money.

He hoped that during the robbery Miss Bancroft would not be in her home, but rather on an errand somewhere.

He looked at his watch. It was 8:20. In exactly one hour, the time lock on the vault would release. If everything went right, less than five minutes after the vault opened, he would be on his way.

He packed his things in his bedroll, picked up his Winchester and descended the stairs to the lobby.

"Checking out?" asked the hotel clerk.

"No, I've decided to stay another couple days," he said as he placed enough money on the counter for two more days lodging.

"Got some business at the bank and some ground to cover in the next few days." That was pretty much the truth, except for the fact that he wasn't coming back.

"I'll be back when I saddle up. Suppose you could rustle up a fresh pot of coffee?"

"Yessir. No problem."

Charles carried his gear to the livery and told the owner to keep some oats on hand, that he would be back in a few days. He saddled his horse and walked him to the far side of the corral where four other horses were already tied to the hitching post. He tied his horse alongside and checked the time. The bank would open in five minutes.

When he returned to the hotel, the coffee was waiting. He sat in the corner where two windows faced both north and west. From here he had a clear view of the streets in all directions, and he could see his horse tied up at the post back of the livery. Directly across he had a view of the bank front.

At exactly 8:45, the teller opened the front door. He came out, looked both ways, stretched, retired inside and closed the door behind him. Moments later, two ladies entered the bank.

A few minutes passed and the same two emerged and walked back from where they came. For the next ten minutes no one entered the bank. Then two men from the direction of the livery crossed the street, both seemingly engaged in heavy conversation as they entered the bank.

A few minutes later another man dressed in a long slicker much like himself came from the direction of the livery and stopped at the steps to the boardwalk. He propped a foot up and fidgeted with his right spur for some time. He then stepped up on the boardwalk leaned against a post and rolled a cigarette.

Charles kept a steady watch through the window. Two men were still inside the bank, and as soon as they came out, he would wander over. Hopefully, by then, the man standing out front would be gone. If not, Charles could outwait him, since he did not have to enter at exactly 9:20.

While he watched, a fourth man came from the east, entered the bank and closed the door. The man on the boardwalk tossed his cigarette in the dirt, straightened up and walked along the facade of the bank, then returned to the end of the boardwalk and remained there.

At that moment Charles saw Miss Constance enter the front door of her living quarters. She must have been down the street earlier, and now was returning home. He did not like that, and thought about changing his escape route.

Charles returned his gaze to the man at the corner of the bank. He had not moved.

Charles glanced at his watch. It was 9:23. He got up from his chair, left the hotel and slowly crossed the street. He had his head down as if not paying attention to anything in particular, but out of the corner of his eye he was watching the man on the steps. The wind whipped a bit and blew the man's slicker aside just for a few seconds, but long enough for Charles to glimpse a pair of cross holsters. Then he noticed the shade of the bank door was drawn shut.

"Don't tell me," he whispered to himself. He felt his nerves jump. He was no more than ten feet away from the steps when the man on the corner stiffened. Charles saw him slowly lower his hand and move his coat behind a revolver. At that moment, the door to the bank jerked open, and one of the men he had spotted earlier stood in the doorway, a sack in one hand, revolver in the other.

"Oh, Lord!" Charles said as he reached for his gun. The man in the long slicker had his revolver out and fired two quick shots, but Charles was already making a dive for cover beneath the front of the boardwalk. Flat on his stomach, and mostly out of sight, he fired at the man on the steps and heard the slug hit him in the chest. He was down.

The man in the doorway fired his revolver, but the shot went wild. Charles leveled his revolver and fired back just as the man shoved the door shut. Charles let loose with two more rounds through the door and heard the man cry out. He must have hit him. His mind was whirling. There were three men—no, four!

At that moment the glass from the front window blew out. Someone had fired a shotgun from inside. Then came a second blast, and buckshot ripped through the front door. More shards of glass flew everywhere, sparkling in the sunlight as if a fireworks display had gone off. The teller inside had come to life, Charles knew as he sprang to the front entrance.

His thoughts suddenly were on Miss Constance. If he himself had planned on exiting the bank through the Bancroft's quarters, these men probably knew the same route. Adrenaline pumped inside him. From within the bank he now heard scuffling and shouting. Two shots rang out, then a third. Moments later two more shots followed and ricocheted, as if off metal. Charles was sure someone had shot the lock off the entrance to the Bancroft's home.

Charles jammed a foot against the bank door, and when it swung open, a slug thumped in the frame above him. He dashed through the opening and immediately tripped over a man lying on the floor. As he went down two more shots rang out, both high above his head.

"Move, dammit, move!" he heard someone shout. Then he heard Miss Bancroft scream out.

Charles scooted across the floor and shoved open the swinging door to the hallway. Two feet away the teller lay face down. Beyond him light poured through the open hallway door. The two men were making their escape through the Bancroft residence.

He jumped to his feet and ran out the front, sure that the two would take Miss Bancroft hostage. He hurried along the outside bank wall, and just as he neared the end, the two men emerged from his right, running as fast as they could across to the corral.

My God, Charles thought. They were running for their horses, which were tied up next to his own!

When the two saw him, they fired at the same time, but they were on the run and their shots struck the bank building behind him.

Charles took careful aim, fired and missed his first shot, then fired again. The nearest man doubled over into the dirt. That was his sixth round.

The one man still running had the sack in his hand and in that sack was Charles' five hundred dollars! Once the man was in the saddle, he cursed at Charles and fired twice at him. But his horse was nervous and crow hopping, and the shots went wild. The man whirled his horse and sped off up the street. Charles ran to his horse, pulled the Winchester from the scabbard and leveled it on the man. He wasn't more than eighty yards away when Charles triggered the rifle.

The man's arms flailed upwards and he somersaulted backwards off his horse as if he were an acrobat. He landed flat on his back in a swirl of dust and didn't move.

It was suddenly very quiet. People were slowly showing up on the streets. An immense relief overcame him when he saw Miss Constance appear at the back door of her home. Seconds later, the Deputy came running up the main street, revolver in hand, and behind him was Mr. Bancroft. The man hadn't even been inside the bank during the robbery.

Someone had summoned a doctor, and within a few minutes two men carried the teller out of the bank. One bullet had gone clean through his left shoulder, another creased his arm, and a third had opened a gash behind his ear. There was hardly a spot on his shirt that was not blood-soaked, but the doctor said he would make it.

Several men gathered up the bodies of the dead men and were lining them up on the boardwalk. A photographer appeared out of nowhere and was in the process of setting up his camera.

Charles stared at the bodies, could hardly believe the scene before him. The first man he had shot took a direct hit in the heart.

The man inside the bank had a load of buckshot in him, delivered by the teller, but he also had been struck in the back by a bullet that pierced his lung and left a gaping hole where it exited his chest. Charles had fired that bullet through the bank door before it struck the man. It had been a blind shot, but a deadly one. If anything, the teller had only hastened the man's death by maybe a half minute.

The man outside near the rear of the bank had taken a bullet, which entered his left side. It had gone clean through his heart and breastbone.

The man who had tried to escape on his horse also met a quick death. The bullet from Charles' Winchester had hit him in the spine in the center of his back.

The deputy's jaw hung open. "I swear, I ain't never seen shootin' like this before."

"How about a picture beside the corpses?" the man with the camera said to Charles.

"What's your name?" asked another.

"He ought to be sheriff," he heard someone else mutter.

Miss Bancroft was in the crowd, her face torn with fear, but he did not speak to her. Instead, he walked slowly back to the hotel while a group of people on his heels congratulated him all the way. He was shaking, and he was sick to his stomach. He had never killed a man before, had no idea he could even kill a man. They had all been lucky shots, and he had delivered them out of desperation to protect Miss Bancroft and her father. What an ironic turn of events. The shootout had lasted no longer than forty-five seconds, a minute at the most.

Charles Hayden remained in town for the better part of a week, just long enough to fill out some paper work for the sheriff. The four men he had killed were known as the Gerard gang, two brothers and two cousins. A five hundred dollar reward on each of their heads was granted to him without question. The amount of the money in the sack, which the robbers had held for so short a time, totaled almost $14,000.00, for which Mr. Bancroft paid a handsome reward to *Charles Howen.*

Charles had intended to split the reward money with the teller, but the doctor had erred in his diagnosis of the man. He bled to death before they could patch him up, and he did not have any living relatives.

The newspaper praised the *"efforts and bravery of Mr. Howen, backed up with a fast gun and a deadly aim."*

A few days later, more articles appeared in the Ogallala newspaper. Journalists reported on the expert shooting of *Mr. Charles Howen* and the keen insight the man had for spotting bank thieves. It was an extraordinary shot he had made with his Winchester when he downed the last man, *"said to be over 300 yards away and shot through the back of the head on the run."*

The papers had made a gunfighter out of him. Charles Hayden was forever grateful all the credit was going to a man named *Charles Howen.*

The offers came in during the few days he remained in Ogallala. Offers for sheriff, a telegraph from Dodge with an offer to be a deputy marshal. Even the railroad had contacted him to represent them as a Pinkerton detective.

And, of course, Mr. Bancroft had made an offer to sell him the range north of town at an ungodly low price, which Charles refused. That was something Mr. Bancroft never understood.

One early morning less than a week after the incident, Charles Hayden packed his belongings on his horse and left the town of Ogallala forever. Many were curious and made inquiry often, wondering where *Charles Howen* had disappeared to, but over the next several months, no information came back. The famous gunfighter had simply vanished. Rumor had it he was killed in Texas by a gunman known as John Wesley Hardin. Another claim stated he had been gunned down in Tucson. One report cited him as alive and well, enjoying a comfortable life as the owner of a general store in Monterey, California. There were those journalists who pursued such rumors in search of the legendary hero, but not for any length of time

Over the next several months, Constance Bancroft received many letters at the post office. On one occasion, the clerk made the mistake of remarking to the young lady that it was strange that none of the letters possessed a return address, to which Miss Constance retorted, "Sir, I do not believe it is any of your business who writes to me."

Within a year, Miss Constance and her father made four trips to Omaha. Everyone in Ogallala assumed they were business trips, but in reality, they were visits to see Charles Hayden. Charles had the utmost admiration for Mr. Bancroft and an amorous interest in Miss Constance, and it was with great humility that he confessed what his initial purpose was in Ogallala.

Quite suddenly, the town of Ogallala discovered it had a new bank owner. It was assumed that Mr. Bancroft and his daughter had moved to Omaha, but eventually, those interested parties discovered that was not the case.

In fact, a few years later, rumor had spread throughout Ogallala that Constance Bancroft had married a Montana rancher by the name of Hayden, and that her father was in business with this man raising horses.

The shootout at the Ogallala Bank was by now practically forgotten, and since neither Mr. Bancroft nor his daughter had near the notoriety that the gunfighter, *Charles Howen*, once possessed, no one really pursued the rumor that the Bancrofts had relocated in Montana. And really, no one cared.

* * *

RUTA'S COMMITMENT

She had met William at a dance in Yankton. Rarely did her parents allow her to participate at such events unchaperoned, but on this July 4th occasion Ruta Bekvar had made the seventeen mile trip along the Missouri River by herself, riding in a two-seater pulled by the family horse.

She stayed with her best friend, Annabelle, who happened to have an invitation that night to meet with her beau, Erik Keller. And it so happened at the evening dance, Erik introduced Ruta to a young man by the name of William Bickford, who, as he himself said, was "traveling through," headed north to the Dakota Territory, to a place called Fargo.

The evening had been grand, especially for Ruta. Ruta fell head over heels in love with William Bickford, the "traveling man" as they all labeled him that night, and each time they did, they laughed and giggled at the moniker attached to him.

William was very good-natured and took the ribbing in style. From the onset, Ruta considered him a handsome sort. He was not much taller than she, but he was very broad shouldered with curly blond hair, and a hint of a smile seemed constant on his rugged and sunburned face. He was a gentleman, so very polite, and was well received by all the young ladies at the party, but he seemed to have singled out this new-found beauty called Ruta. She was a charm, danced beautifully and talked like an educated young lady, and well schooled, he was sure, to more than the average extent.

She hoped to be a musician. He hoped to own half of Dakota Territory by the time he was fifty, to which everyone applauded good-naturedly.

He was so enthralled with Ruta, that he stayed an extra day before he headed north. And of course, he spent almost every hour of it with her, chaperoned by Annabelle.

He moved on, much to the sorrow of Ruta. Two months later Erik and Annabelle were married, and on the very day of the event, Ruta received a letter from Fargo.

Every two weeks after that, a letter arrived at the post office for her, and she wrote back as often as he wrote. After several months of exchanging letters, William Bickford offered a proposal of marriage, and Ruta wrote back that she would accept. Her parents could not believe she would entertain the proposal. The two had endured virtually no courtship period, and her parents threatened they would disown her. But Ruta was a stern woman, a young lady of commitment, and less than a week later both parents saw her off at the stage.

The Yankton stage went only as far as Sioux Falls, a mere 70 miles. From there the only stage route to Fargo was by way of Minneapolis, an extra 250 miles out of the way, or an additional four day trip. Being a practical lady, Ruta inquired around town and located a freighter headed north to Fargo. She talked the driver into taking her along for just a few dollars. When she reached Fargo, she had word sent to William Bickford that she had arrived. She waited in the lobby of the Fargo Hotel, one of the few structures, which lined Front Street, and by late afternoon William arrived in a buckboard. He was wearing a new black suit and a derby. When he first saw her, he whirled her around and around and kissed her for the longest time as a small crowd of onlookers cheered.

By five o'clock, William had found a pastor, and they were married. After the ceremony, a few of William's friends celebrated with them over a fine meal of prairie chicken.

They spent their wedding night in the same hotel, and though

Ruta had known her husband, actually had only *seen him*, for the better part of two days within the last ten months, it was a night that would trigger memories for years to come. He was ever so gentle with her, and if she had any sense of guilt or shame in undressing before him, it all disappeared in what she considered an evening of absolute bliss.

In the morning, after a hearty breakfast, the two headed north along the Red River toward the acreage William had purchased. Actually, land in the Dakota Territory was given gratis by the government to any person who farmed and maintained 160 acres for five consecutive years. So, William was in the process of "proving up," as the process was labeled.

Along the twenty five-mile route, Ruta marveled at the bareness of the landscape. In Yankton, the hills, too, were rolling, but trees seemed to line every creek and river, and it was not unusual to find large groves of trees here and there, especially in the valley surrounding the town.

This Dakota Territory was indeed the open prairie, most of it flat with some low rolling hills, but once away from the rivers, a tree was hard to find.

But Ruta, not yet twenty, was a woman of conviction. She had made up her mind well ahead of time that when she married, it would be "for better or for worse," just like the pastor had said at the wedding ceremony. She was known as a lady who followed through whenever she made a commitment.

She had endured the long trip to Fargo over the objection of her parents and had married a man she had known for only a few days. She had not been disappointed so far, and she was not going to let a barren prairie get the best of her.

But when the buggy dipped over the last ridge of the twenty five mile trip, and she saw for the first time what William Bickford considered their new home, she shrank back in wonderment. The front was a hodgepodge of clapboard and wood, covered with black tar paper. The back of the home receded into a hill of dirt, which offered space enough for an additional room. The entire inside wasn't much more than twenty by twenty feet. It was a far cry from the home she had grown up in near Yankton, a two-story affair with her own bedroom.

William stood proudly before the structure. "I built it by myself," he said. "That's why I couldn't come and get you. I wanted it finished before you arrived."

She entered the interior and looked around. "It has everything I imagined," she answered with a broad smile as truthfully as she could. It had a narrow bed at one end of the room, a stove and table with two chairs, and a few shelves, which represented the cupboard. On the shelves were canned goods, flour, salt, all the staples necessary for making at least the barest of meals. She stared at a floor, which was nothing more than packed dirt, and she wondered if she swept it often enough, would the floor eventually work its way into the ground?

The home did not remotely resemble the sort of living quarters she had expected, not that she expected elegance. But a structure of this nature in Yankton would be judged as living quarters for the extremely poor.

William was a proud man, proud of the quarters he had built, and proud of the makeshift corral which contained his two work horses and riding horse. When she considered what material was available in this god-forsaken land, she too had to confess, at least to herself, it was a rather remarkable accomplishment.

Ruta accepted the situation and started off her new home with the best intentions.

By June first, less than a month after she had arrived, she had a complete garden underway with corn, squash, watermelons, tomatoes, and a large patch of potatoes.

The garden did well that season, and so did William's crop of wheat and corn. The first winter was fairly mild for these parts, not much more than three feet of snow during the entire season, but still the winter days seemed to drag by. Rarely did anyone visit, nor did they travel anywhere. The weather was entirely too unpredictable.

The following spring, the two were at work again with the plowing and planting and gardening. Occasionally neighbors dropped in from miles away, which was always a welcome gesture, and a grand departure from the extreme monotony Ruta was now experiencing.

But perseverance was a large part of her makeup, and she never let on for a moment that she was unhappy. During the first year, she had made only one trip to Fargo with William. That was basically for supplies. They stayed one night and were back on the trail headed for home early the next day.

Two more years passed, and one day while William was plowing, she saw a wagon appear on the horizon, ambling down toward the farm. By the time the wagon rolled to a stop, William had run back from the field to meet the driver. The somewhat bulky item in the back of the dray, covered with a tarp, had already peaked her curiosity. William was as excited as she had ever seen him when he threw back the covering.

He watched her face glow as she stared at the piano.

"It is so beautiful, William." Tears ran down her face, she was so overcome with emotion. She had missed her music, and she had talked about how it would be nice to have a piano. But she never imagined she would ever have a piano here, miles from nowhere.

"It will give you something to do this winter," he said.

She looked at the size of the piano, then at the clapboard hut. "Where are we going to keep it?"

He was ever so smug. "We'll make room. In a few days, I have a load of lumber coming, so we can start building a new house."

Her jaw dropped.

The lumber arrived less than a week later, and by October, William and a few neighbors had put up most of the structure. Another mild winter allowed William to continually work at the home, each day ending with another small portion of the interior more livable. By January, they had transferred everything from the clapboard-soddy to the new home. William had acquired another riding horse, and now the horses and a few pigs, which they had been raising, had better quarters than the small lean-to he had tacked on to the former house.

The trees they had planted that first summer were creating a shelter of their own, gaining prominence against the bitter winter north winds. News had spread that Ruta had a piano, and that alone enticed neighbors to make an extra effort to travel as much as fifteen miles, simply to hear her play.

She practiced almost every day, and when she had free time, she took to riding the extra horse, since that spring William had bought her a new saddle.

After five years, the acreage belonged to them. One hundred sixty acres of proved-up land. They both traveled to Fargo to collect the deed, a momentous occasion, and for both, quite an achievement.

Life was, for the most part, good for them. But in these short five years of making a living and improving the farm, Ruta had not been able to bear a child. It was the topic of conversation, it seemed at every evening meal. Over the period of the last year or so, Ruta almost hated to prepare supper, knowing William would again and again bring up the topic of children. It had become an obsession, and he began to lament, and made excuses when he went to bed, that he was too tired to make love to her like he had so often done before.

Finally, one evening during their meal, William stomped out of the home, yelling as he went, "Why can't you have children like any other normal woman!"

They continued to work together, day by day, always making improvements on the farm, but they grew apart in terms of the love they once shared for each other. During the days when William was at work in the field, Ruta would cry, sometimes for hours at a time. Yet, before William returned, she always managed to regain her composure, for she still loved him, and she was sure he loved her, inwardly. It was always the question of children, and now she had fears that she herself was infertile. She had, on rare occasion, talked to a few of the neighbor ladies about her condition, and though some remedies were suggested, any attempts changed nothing.

Their love-making had all but stopped over a period of several months. Though William now refrained from even mentioning children, she knew he was suffering inside with a burden beyond description. He never struck her, or even hinted at physically abusing her, but being shunned was enough abuse, and Ruta had become as distressed as she had ever been about her future with this man.

News of the Fourth of July celebration in Fargo had spread far in advance, and though William was behind in his work, he consented to take Ruta. It was a full day event, so the two packed up their buggy and left early in the morning. William had not spoken much during the trip to Fargo, but once there, the celebrating took on a renewed sense of encouragement. The two ate well, met old friends and danced late into the night. It was reminiscent of the first time the two had met in Yankton. William had had a few more drinks than usual and was feeling very contented, and even boasted about what a wonderful wife he had.

That evening, after more drinking and celebrating, William and Ruta spent the night in the very same hotel where they had consummated their marriage some six years before. William was amorous, and Ruta was receptive.

For a month or so after that day, William seemed to be in a much better mood, and the two talked about making another effort at having children, and they made love often.

The crops were good that summer, and they fared well on the farm. This was their sixth year of marriage, and late in that summer, Ruta received a letter from home stating that her mother was ill. In all this time, she had not once visited her parents in the Czech community of Yankton. When she asked if she and William could afford a visit, William was for it, but the timing was not good for him. He had planned on building a granary and new barn before the summer crop was in. The lumber had been ordered, and men had been commissioned to help him build it.

Ruta suggested that if he could not take the time to travel to Yankton, would he care if she went alone?

"That's a long trip, Ruta," he told her. "Do you feel up to it?"

She retorted, "I made the trip by myself to marry you, William. I'm sure I can make the trip by myself again. And besides, I'll be taking the train to Sioux Falls." In the past year, the railroad had opened a line between Fargo and Sioux Falls. She would still have to take the stage from Sioux Falls to Yankton.

It was decided. A few days later, he took her to Fargo. During the way they talked a lot, and William was in a good mood when he saw her off at the depot.

Ruta was full of excitement. There were a lot of friends and acquaintances to visit with once she returned.

She had heard often from her friend, Annabelle. She and her husband, Erik, now an up and coming banker, had four children, three boys and a girl. It would be so good to see them, to see how the Keller family had grown, to catch up on all the news...and gossip! And of course, to visit her own family.

* * *

Almost a full month passed until Ruta returned. Her mother had taken a turn for the better, which helped make the trip most memorable. On the way back, all went well, except for a two-day delay when exceptionally high water had washed the ferry downstream on the James River, preventing the stage from crossing. Less than a week after that when she arrived in Fargo, William was waiting at the depot, and he was in a most jovial mood, and so happy to see her.

"You can't imagine how tough it's been to have to make my own meals," he joked "And the piano needs some attention!" He whirled her around and gave her a big kiss.

Before they left town, William escorted her to a dress shop and had her pick out any new dress she wanted. He waited patiently in the outer lobby while she tried on a few and even helped her with the final selection.

Ruta had missed William terribly and was so happy to return.

They headed home in a new buggy, which William had acquired only that day. It was a surrey, with a canvas top and side covers, so that during a rain they could remain fairly dry. This was a wonderful improvement over the flat wagon box they had. They kept the wagon box, of course, for hauling supplies, but this surrey was pure luxury!

When they rode over the final ridge to the home place, Ruta gasped at the new structures. The barn was two stories with a haymow, and the granary was huge. Alongside the granary William had also built a small machine shop.

When William stopped the surrey in front of the house and helped Ruta down from the rig, he was grinning from ear to ear, and she knew he had something else planned. When she entered the home, she was speechless with wonderment.

"It's called wallpaper," William told her. "What do you think?"

Ruta held her tiny hands up to her face and gasped. She had heard of the decorative paper, had seen it in hotel lobbies. Every wall was covered with green and yellow flowers. The living room, the kitchen, the bedroom, the storage room—everything green and yellow!

"I just love it!" she cried out. Her initial reaction was *beautiful*. But, to cover every square inch with the same paper seemed a bit much, yet, she held her tongue. In time, she would suggest other patterns.

Life had made a better turn for both of them, and for the next few weeks, the two fell into a daily routine that kept them busy. Barely a month had gone by when Ruta noticed a change in her body. She had not had the normal few days of the monthly curse, and though she was sure she knew the reason, she let another month go by until, one evening at mealtime, she broke the news to her husband.

"I believe we're with child," she said as he was spooning up a mouthful of stew.

"We're what?" he asked.

"I'm going to have a baby!" she said as she ran her hands

over her stomach. She was not at all large in any sense of the word, but William was ecstatic with the news, and he felt her stomach with his own hands, even leaned his ear down to listen if he could detect any movement inside.

Immediately, he wanted her to rest, to at least sit down while he washed up the dishes. She must not spend time playing the piano, nor go for long walks. "And you must not work in the garden!" he scolded.

She laughed, reminded him it was November, and that the garden had already suffered a first mild frost.

She had never seen him so happy, not since the first few years of their marriage. He was so thrilled it was all he could talk about. When it came time, a neighbor lady was present to help with the delivery.

They named him Aaron Samuel Bickford. Aaron was her father's name, Samuel was his father's name.

This first child for William was a good omen, and three years later, when Ruta was 31 years old, she gave birth to a second child, which they named Annabelle, after her best friend in Yankton.

Ruta was a wonderful wife to her husband, and William loved her more than anything in the world.

The ranch prospered even more, and William was a wonderful father to the children, just as he was a wonderful husband to Ruta. Over the years they acquired more than three thousand acres, and for the last several years of his life, William had invested wisely in cattle.

Aaron took over the ranch since he possessed a similar dream like his father's. Their daughter, Annabelle, became a family doctor, a very rare occupation for a woman in the early 1900's.

William died when he was 68 years old, with Ruta by his bedside. She loved him to the very last minute, and was holding his hand when he took his last breath.

Ruta was a most devoted woman, a lady of conviction, and she could not have found a more loving man with whom to spend a lifetime.

She had shared every day of her life loving William and had kept but one secret from him. During their lifetime, she and William had traveled to Yankton to visit on several occasions. But there were those times when Ruta made the trip alone, especially during busy seasons when William could not get away. Not once had he ever put the facts together, that shortly after she returned from these trips to Yankton, she had announced she was pregnant.

She dared not name their first born Erik, but when the girl came along, she felt relatively secure in naming her Annabelle. It was extremely strange. Her best friend, Annabelle, and her husband, Erik, had agreed to the consensual, highly unusual, yet practical solution to the happiness of William and Ruta.

It was a secret, which Ruta could never confess to William.

After William died, the guilt of what she had done turned to shame, and for weeks she lamented over the fact she had never told him. She did not dare, for she knew it would have ruined their life together, and she loved William so much that she could not bear to live without him.

Sometime later when she was going through his desk discarding items that were of no value, she came across a letter addressed to her in her husband's handwriting. It was a simple note:

> *My dearest Ruta,*
> *I have known for years that I was not the father of our children. I am so deeply sorry I could not bring myself to tell you of it, but I feared if I did, it would shame you so much you might leave me, and I could not imagine living without you. Now that I am gone, it is our secret, and Aaron and Annabelle shall always be our children. I never needed to forgive you, for there was nothing to forgive.*
> *Your loving husband, William*

For the next nine years, Ruta lived a life of contentment and good conscience. One beautiful, June afternoon while playing the piano, she simply slumped forward and died.

* * *

RUSTLER'S BLUFF

"You sent for me, sir?" asked Wade Hendricks. He was standing in front of Harmon Russell's desk in the drawing room of his lavish ranch home. Wade had only been inside the home once before. As he looked around, he admired the fancy stuffed chairs and the leather couch. Various trophies adorned almost every space on the walls. Directly behind Harmon Russell's desk on the wall was a gun collection made up of vintage weapons of the late 1700's and early 1800's.

Harmon Russell spun his chair half way around, wrinkled up his face and dipped his bushy white eyebrows. "Lefty got himself beat up last night at the Longhorn. I suppose you heard about that?" said Russell.

"Yessir."

Lefty Ingstrom was Russell's foreman, his right hand man in almost all matters dealing with the HR Ranch. "He's got a broken arm and a fractured jaw. He ain't going to be worth a damn to me for a couple months."

"Yessir. Ah, no sir," Wade corrected himself. He wasn't sure what Mr. Russell was leading up to.

"I was going to send Lefty down to Abilene with 300 cattle next week."

"Yessir."

"Think you can ramrod those cattle down for me?"

Wade gulped. "Yessir."

"Take those two yayhoo buddies of yours along."

"Yessir. They're both in town at the moment, sir."

Harmon Russell's bushy eyebrows jumped. "What the hell they doin' there?"

"Lefty gave them the day off today, sir. We all been working pretty much every day this month. I was supposed to get tomorrow off."

"Well, you're leaving tomorrow, so look's like your day off will have to wait."

Wade didn't have a choice. "Yessir, that's no problem, sir. But I thought you were going to send the herd next week."

"There's a shortage of beef right now and if I can beat those drovers coming up from Texas, I can get fifty dollars for each cow. That's eight dollars more a head than I could get last week. Know how much three hundred head will bring?"

"Ahh..."

"Fifteen thousand dollars," finished Russell.

"I was just going to say that," answered Wade.

"Eight dollars more a head means twenty four hundred dollars more profit. But that price ain't goin' to last. You got ten days to get that herd down to Abilene, you understand?"

"That's 150 miles from here, Mr. Russell. Ellsworth would be a lot closer."

"What are you, some kind of geographer?"

"No sir."

"You're going to Abilene because that's where I cut the deal. Got that straight?"

"Yessir," said Wade. Fifteen miles a day was an awfully fast pace for a herd, he was thinking. Ten was even pushing it. "What about a cook and someone to handle the string of horses?"

Harmon Russell did a lot of talking just with his bushy eyebrows, and now they dipped into a mean scowl. That meant Wade had just asked a dumb question.

"I'll have some of the hands cut out the herd at Slocums Creek this afternoon," said Russell. "Tomorrow morning draw five days grub from Corky."

"Only five?"

"Damn. I got to spell out everything for you? Halfway down to Abilene, stop at Calley's Station and pick up grub for the rest of the trip." He stood up as if his instructions were over, and then he added, "Ride into town and find Pinky and Custer, then hightail it back here. And by god, those two yayhoos better be sober!"

"Yessir."

Wade Hendricks made his way out the door before Harmon Russell gave him a chance to ask some more dumb questions. His horse was right outside, and in seconds he was in the saddle heading for town.

Pinky and Custer were in the Longhorn Saloon, the same place Lefty had been beat to a pulp the day before. When he located them, they were at a table by themselves with an empty bottle and two empty glasses in front of them.

Pinky was of slim build, wiry and had a scraggly beard on his gaunt face. He had picked up the nickname Pinky long ago, because the skin on his face was naturally red. He was a good drinker and a poor gambler.

Custer was a little heavy set, always wore a plaid green shirt, always wore suspenders, which held up a gray pair of canvas trousers left over from the Civil War. The war had been five years in passing, and Custer was long overdue for a new pair of pants. He too, was a good drinker, but spent most of his money on the ladies, for which he received very little in return.

Of the three, Wade was the neatest. His attire always consisted of a colorful shirt and a black vest and black pants. The three had punched cattle in Tennessee and Arkansas, and last year they had helped bring a herd of cattle up from Austin, Texas. In that sense, they were rounders, all in their mid twenties, all broke most of the time. The three wore six-shooters on their hips, but nothing fancy.

"Boys," said Wade as he sat down at the table. "You can't guess what just happened."

"Russell done keeled over from a heart attack," said Pinky.

"Nope," said Wade.

"One of the boys shot him in the back," said Custer.

Wade laughed out loud. Harmon Russell was a hard man to work for, and the boys were always spoofing, hoping some terrible disaster would befall the rancher.

"You boys heard about Lefty, I suppose."

"Hell, we was here last night when the Bar L boys kicked the shit out of him," said Pinky. "That Lefty just don't know when to keep his mouth shut. Someone said ol' Russell was a mean sum-na-bitch, and dumb Lefty stuck up fer him agin'."

"Lefty's still over at the Doc's," added Custer. "He ain't in any workin' condition."

"That's why I'm here," said Wade. "Russell was going to send Lefty down to Abilene with a herd of cattle next week, and just a half hour ago he asked me if I'd take them down."

Pinky's and Custer's mouths dropped.

"He told me to get hold of my yayhoo buddies, meaning you two. He's asking us three to make the drive."

"Who the hell's he think he is calling us yayhoos?" asked Pinky.

"Yeah," added Custer. Let the ol' fart take his own cattle down. We don't need to be insulted like that."

"He ain't got anybody else to send. Curly, Brad and Forest ain't been ramrodding for Russell as long as we been. Don't you see? Russell might be a son-of-a-bitch, but at least he picked us cause we been on the payroll longer than the others."

Pinky's red face lit up even redder. "Hey," he said as he hunkered down at the table and looked around to see if anybody was listening. "We talked about running off with some of his cattle a'fore, didn't we?"

"Well, I'll be," said Custer as his mind began to clear.

"You boys got it." said Wade. We been talking about rustlin' some of his cattle for months, and now he's giving us a herd of 300 cattle to run down to Abilene."

"What's the plan?" asked Pinky.

"We head out in the morning, run the cattle down like he said, pick up the cash, and instead of puttin' it in the bank, we put it in our pockets and head back to Texas."

"Now, that there is a real plan," said Pinky.

"Russell said the cattle price is up. That means fifty dollars a head times three hundred. Figure it out."

Both Pinky and Custer threw back their heads as if they were calculating, but neither of them could add or subtract, so multiplication was far beyond them.

"That's fifteen thousand dollars," said Wade.

"I was just goin' to say that," affirmed Pinky.

"Well, I'll be whupsnockered," said Custer. "I could get some new clothes."

"So, do we do it?" asked Wade. Both nodded their heads enthusiastically. "What do you say we drink on it?"

"Good idea," said Custer. "You got any money?"

* * *

They were four days on the trail, moving the herd as fast as they could. Three hundred was not a lot of cattle for a trail drive, but going was slow without a cook and a wrangler to handle the six additional horses in the remuda. They had to double up on chores, which kept them busy every minute of the day. They figured they had made about forty-five miles in four days, but according to Russell's schedule, they were already one day behind. It was hot, the cattle were moody, and the only respite came in the evening when the night air cooled down.

Pinky was flanking one side of the herd, Wade the other, Custer was bringing up the drag. He had more dust on him then a dead horse in a sawmill. "Damn, " he cussed as he snapped his lariat at the heels of the lagging cows. "These four-legged critters look like they're ready for a nap. I'm tired and I'm hungry."

Since they had no chuckwagon, the three had been carrying their food in their bedrolls, and after four days almost everything was gone. Russell had given Wade fifteen dollars to restock at Rube Calley's Station, a little trading post in the middle of nowhere. Wade figured they were ten or twelve miles southwest of the station. He rode over to Custer. "You and Pinky keep the herd moving for another couple hours. I'll ride over to Calley's place and get some more grub."

"Might not hurt to pick up a bottle or two of hooch while you're at it," said Custer.

Wade didn't answer, just stuck his spurs at his horse and jumped his bay into a nice lope. The three had enough on their hands driving the cattle sober, let alone drunk. The drinking would have to wait until they reached the cattle-pens at Abilene.

As Wade rode along, he noticed the clouds building up in the northwest. He knew a rainstorm was coming for sure, but he hoped it wasn't a thunderstorm. Two men trying to contain three hundred head under those conditions was a mean task.

It took an hour to reach Calley's creek, and when he did, he wasn't sure if he was north or south of the trading post. He picked south and rode for a couple miles, and when he discovered he should have gone the other way, rain was already coming down. He pulled his slicker from his roll, slapped it on and nudged his horse a bit faster. By the time he caught sight of trading post, the rain was coming down ferociously, and the sky was practically black. Calley had a lean-to on the south side of his station. Two horses were tied to a rail, so Wade tied his horse next to them, pulled some hay down from a loft for his bay and went inside.

Rube Calley was sitting at a table with two other men. "Howdy, Wade. What the hell brings you out in this hurricane?"

"Poor judgment," said Wade. "Me, Pinky and Custer are moving a small herd. I need grub for the three of us, six or seven day's worth."

"You got it," said Rube. He went behind the counter and began rustling up the food.

"Pushin' on down to Ellsworth, are ya?" asked one of the two men at the table. The man that spoke was a heavy-set fellow with a fat face under a scrubby beard. He was wearing a dirty, red and white polka dot shirt that should have been thrown away a year ago. He had on a buckskin jacket, which covered most of it, and his hat was turned up in the front like a Mexican sombrero.

"Nope, Abilene," said Wade.

"Picked a horseshit day to do it."

"I reckon you're right, but then, it wasn't my pickin'," said Wade.

They all laughed over that.

The other man was smaller, dressed in a long black coat. He had thick, black eyebrows and a long pointed nose, which made him look like a weasel. "If'n there's only three of you fellers, you can't be moving too many head."

"Three hundred," said Wade.

"Ooh, that's a fair size fer only three," said the little guy.

"Well, hell," said the fat man as he got up and walked behind the bar to get a shot glass. "Man who risks his hide in this miserable weather deserves a drink." He poured a shot for Wade.

"Thank you, friend," said Wade. The rain was now coming down in buckets. He didn't think a duck would go out in this weather, and he was concerned about Pinky and Custer. He hoped they had bedded down the cattle before the storm hit. There wasn't much sense in returning until the rain abated, so Wade chatted some more with the two strangers and Rube.

The fat man poured Wade another drink, and another, and another.

When Wade woke, his head felt like it was in a bucket of cement. A lone candle vaguely lit up the interior of the post. The clock indicated it was three a.m.

The two strangers were gone, but Wade could hear Rube snoring away from an adjacent room. Wade stumbled to his feet, gathered up the sack of grub and went outside. A quarter moon gave just enough light for him to see what he doing, although he wasn't seeing very well at all.

He hooked the sack of goods on his saddle, climbed on his horse and headed back along the creek. It was cold for a spring morning. The rain had quit, but now a cloud layer was once again moving in, and before long it was totally dark.

He wandered around heading in what he thought was a southwesterly direction. On the way in, he had kept track of some landmarks, but now he could hardly make out anything within fifty yards. His horse was doing fine, and he regretted he couldn't just tell him to find the herd.

He continued to amble along, half asleep in the saddle and half drunk. His head was not clear enough to think up an excuse to give Pinky and Custer, and they were sure to ask him why he was so late. The boys would be hungry by now, but he rationalized that even if he had returned the evening before, it would have rained so hard they wouldn't have been able to start a fire to cook a meal.

By daybreak, he was finally beginning to focus a bit on the terrain, but nothing looked familiar. He knew they had crossed a creek sometime before he left the herd, but he had not yet come to a creek. He finally rode to the top of the highest hill he could find and then scanned every direction. Off to the south he spotted two horses grazing. Feeling some relief, he rode in that direction and discovered the two horses were from the remuda, but there were no cattle around, nothing to suggest he was even near the herd. He figured the two must have wandered off, so he tethered them together with his lasso, picked south as his best guess and rode off.

Inside of an hour, he came over a rise to find Pinky and Custer on foot, heading in his direction. All they were carrying was their Winchester rifles.

"Where the devil you been?" Pinky hollered out when they were in earshot.

Wade's mouth hung open. "Where's the herd?"

Custer threw up his hands. "Gone."

"What the hell do you mean, gone?"

"We had the cattle bedded down when the rain hit, and was waiting on you under some trees. Then all hell broke loose. A'fore we know'd it, we heard gunshots and the cattle was on the run."

"What do you mean, gunshots?" asked Wade.

"What we got to do to unrattle your brain?" asked Custer. "Beat you with a stick?"

"We was rustled," added Pinky. "Some fellers done rustled Russell's cattle."

Wade was dumbfounded. "Where's your horses?"

"Gone with the rest of em'," said Custer. He looked at the two horses behind Wade. "Cep'n for those two. "Our saddles are back yonder a couple miles where we made camp."

"Which way did the cattle go?"

"Danged if we know. It was darker than your head in a flour sack at midnight. They was headed south, but by now they could be scattered all over Kansas."

Pinky and Custer makeshifted some bridles and climbed on the two spare horses. In short time they reached the place where they had camped, ate some food, put the saddles on the horses and headed south looking for the herd. They split up a mile apart, each looking for traces of the cattle. If someone found them, he was to fire three shots but by late afternoon they came together without any luck.

"Nothin'," said Pinky. "If'n we don't get these cattle back, Mr. Russell'l be mad enough to swallow a horned toad backwards."

"Pinky, you're dumber than a dead coyote," said Custer. "We ain't lookin' for the herd to give it back to Russell. We're lookin' to get it back for us. We're the ones that been rustled."

Pinky thought a moment. "Right."

Wade was looking over the lay of the land. They had covered several miles to the south with no luck. Though it appeared the cattle were headed south, it made sense that the rustlers wouldn't be heading for any of the cattle towns. They would take a different direction, more than likely west or back north.

"Let's go west," said Wade. "Spread out like we done before. We'll ride until nightfall."

When the sun went down, they still had not located any trace of the herd. That night they camped alongside a narrow creek, and by sunup they had cooked a hot meal of beans, and washed them down with hot coffee. Once again in the saddle, they spread out and headed west again.

By midday they found the trail of the herd. They figured they were at least thirty miles to the southwest of where the rustlers had struck.

"How the hell'd they get this far?" asked Pinky.

"I'm guessing the cattle stampeded and ran probably ten miles in the night," said Wade. "They gotta be pushing them hard. Could be another fifteen or twenty miles ahead."

The three urged their horses into a lope following the trail. The thieves were keeping to the draws and low side of the hills, zigzagging every now and then to the north, and then back west again. Wade figured the rustlers knew this territory well.

Inside of an hour, they caught sight of the herd. On top of a knoll, the three lay on their bellies watching the rustlers drive the cattle below them. The remuda was moving along with them, although two of the horses were missing. More than likely some of the cattle, too, had been lost during the stampede. There were six men in all, pushing the cattle hard, all wearing hardware on their hips, all carrying Winchesters on their saddles.

Good god, thought Wade to himself when the rider nearest him shucked his buckskin jacket and tied it on behind. He was wearing a loud, red and white polka dot shirt! Looking over the other men, Wade spotted the other weasel-like character. These were the two who had got him drunk at Calley's Trading Post. "Damn, I been bamboozled," said Wade.

"What's that?" asked Custer.

"Nothing." Wade wasn't about to confess his stupidity to Custer and Pinky.

"I say we shoot 'em dead," said Pinky. "There ain't nothin' worse than a thievin' rustler."

"Let's not be too hasty with the talk, Pinky," said Custer. "You sort of forget what we was doin' before these rustlers done rustled us."

The one thing Wade wanted to avoid was gunplay. He himself wasn't a good shot, and he knew for sure Pinky and Custer couldn't hit the side of a barn even if they were shooting from inside.

Wade looked toward the south and estimated they weren't any more than fifty miles from Ellsworth. It suddenly came to him. "Remember a couple years back in Ellsworth, we all got drunk in Birdie's Saloon?"

"I remember we all got in a hell of a fight," said Custer.

"You remember Joe Purdy?"

"Holy b'jeez," said Custer. "Ain't no one in a hundred miles around don't know that scoundrel. He'd kill his own mother for a five dollar gold piece."

Wade didn't think Joe Purdy ever had a mother. There wasn't a more hot-tempered cowboy on the circuit. In the last six years, Joe Purdy had been beaten up in every saloon from Sedalia to Ellsworth. He had been in a half dozen gunfights and had as many holes in him to prove it.

Wade went on. "Well, I saved his ass that night from getting a .45 slug through his brain, and he said if I ever needed a favor, I was to call on him. His place is about ten miles south of here." He looked right into Custer's face. "You go find Joe Purdy and tell him Wade said it's payback time. Dig up as many riders as you can, make sure they all got carbines, and get on back here pronto."

Wade was thrilled with his plan. When Joe Purdy and his bunch showed up, these rustlers were in for it. One mention of Joe Purdy's name and the thieves would high-tail it faster than a jackrabbit with a pack of wolves in pursuit.

"And then are we goin' to shoot 'em dead?" asked Pinky.

Wade took in a deep breath. Pinky was as good at dumb thinking as he was at gambling. "Dammit, Pinky, we ain't killers and we ain't gunfighters. All we need is a show of force. Custer, you take Pinky with you. If you ride hard, you can be back before sundown. They'll probably keep pushing the herd west, so keep that in mind on your return trip. I'll be looking for you. Now scoot, the both of you."

The two jumped on their horses and took off. Wade returned to the top of the hill and watched as the rustlers continued to push the herd onward. He could hardly wait until Custer and Pinky returned. Before the day was over, there was going to be a showdown.

But come sundown, Custer and Pinky were nowhere in sight. Wade spent the night on the open prairie two miles south of the herd. He didn't dare light a fire, and cursed that he had to eat cold beans and tack.

By sunup he was cursing more, wondering what happened to Custer and Pinky. The rustlers were again moving the cattle in a westerly direction, and by late afternoon, they turned directly south, driving the cattle along the bottom of a deep draw.

Finally, on the horizon, Wade caught sight of a bunch of riders coming his way. He quickly mounted and rode to meet the group, but as he neared them, his jaw dropped.

"H'lo, Wade," offered Custer.

Wade couldn't believe the weather-beaten group in front of him. Custer and Pinky brought back eight men, half of them dressed in bib overalls and floppy hats, the others in an assortment of ragged shirts and pants. Two of them were kids, no more than eleven or twelve years old. Hanging behind them was a mangy looking black dog, gray from age and with one leg limping.

"Where the hell is Joe Purdy?" asked Wade.

"Kilt," said Custer. "Two months ago someone shot-gunned

him in Ellsworth. Got one of his brothers, too, and the other one high-tailed it. Ain't no Purdy boys around nowheres."

Wade carefully examined the bunch. Two of the men had old cap and ball sidearms, one had a Sharps single shot, another had a double barrel shotgun. The rest didn't have any weapons. And not one of them remotely resembled a gunfighter.

Custer and Pinky could see the disillusionment on Wade's face.

"We done the best we could," said Pinky.

"What am I going to do with this group?"

"Well," said Custer, "you said you wanted a show of force. These boys are up here to help us with our cattle problem."

One of the riders nudged his horse forward. "I'm Zeb Hanska." His speech was slow and drawled out. "These are my brothers Lem and Pete, my two boys and some neighbor friends. We've moved cattle a'fore, and we won't shirk our responsibilities. Just tell us what we got to do and we'll do it."

Wade looked at Custer and Pinky. "You told these men they were to help us move cattle?"

Neither answered, simply lowered their heads.

Zeb spoke again. "We understand a thunderstorm scattered your herd. We'll help you gather them, collect our fee and be on our way."

"What fee?"

Custer cringed. "I promised them all five dollars apiece."

"Five dollars!? For what?"

"To help round up your cattle," said Zeb. He spat out a big gob of brown goo on the ground.

Custer fidgeted in his saddle. "We didn't exactly tell em' the truth."

"We done the best we could," Pinky repeated.

Zeb was as confused as anyone in his group. "What seems to be the problem?"

Wade was thinking, five dollars apiece meant forty dollars total, practically two month's wages. He walked his horse in front of the lined up men, sizing them up. With his arm pointed toward the west, he said very calmly, "'Bout two miles away over that ridge are six rustlers driving our herd. We'd like to get our cattle back."

Zeb scowled. "Rustlers you say? We ain't for gunplay, you understand."

"I can see that."

"Are they well-armed?"

"They all have sidearms and Winchesters."

Zeb looked at the double-barrel he was carrying. "I don't believe we are any match for them."

"No, I don't think you are."

"Well, we done tried to accommodate you," said Zeb almost apologetically, "but it didn't work out, so we'll just be on our way."

"Wait!" said Wade. "Don't you want to make your five dollars apiece?"

"We ain't gunfighters, sir," answered Zeb. "We don't cotton to goin' up against rustlers or otherwise."

"I ain't asking you to get in a shoot-out."

Zeb held up his horse. "Then what are you asking, sir?"

Wade hesitated, then said, "I'm just looking for... a show of force."

"Sorry," said Zeb. "We ain't no show of force."

Wade had a plan, but the sun was getting low in the sky. "All you got to do is line up your horses on that far ridge." Wade pointed across a draw. "Get on the west side and be in place when the sun starts going down. Custer and Pinky will go with you."

Zeb didn't seem interested.

"I'll give you ten dollars a man," Wade quickly added.

Zeb raised an eyebrow, looked back at his brothers. Both shook their heads.

"Guess not," answered Zeb.

"I'm only asking for about thirty minutes of your time."

Zeb looked back at his brothers. Same answer.

Wade was quick to respond. "Twenty-five dollars a man!"

Custer and Pinky stirred in their saddles.

At the same time Zeb's eyes lit up. "For the young'ens, too?" he asked.

"For the young'ens, too."

"You got that much cash on you, sir?" he asked.

"No," said Wade. "But after we get rid of these thievin' rustlers, you can pick out any four cows you want. They're worth fifty
dollars a head in Abilene."

Lem and Pete nodded their approval.

Wade felt a huge relief, but he knew he wasn't out of the
bear's den yet. They all listened carefully to Wade's instructions,
and when he finished they rode off in the direction he had indicated
earlier, the mangy dog lagging far behind.

Twenty minutes later Wade was in position. He had seen his
group of men ride out of sight to the south, and in a few minutes
more they should be on the other side of the draw and ahead of the
herd.

With a white handkerchief tied to the barrel of his Winchester, he rode over the top of the rise in plain sight of the two rustlers
closest to him below. One of them was the fellow in the red and
white polka dot shirt. Surprisingly, Wade had made it half way down
the side of the hill before the polka dot rustler saw him. The big
man, suddenly startled, pulled his pistol out and pointed it at Wade.

"Howdy," said Wade as he rode up to the man and stopped
his horse. The weasel-like character rode over from the other side of
the herd, and within seconds the other rustlers began riding in his
direction.

"Well, don't that beat all," said the man in the red and white
shirt. He quickly scanned the ridges around him and then looked
Wade directly in the eyes. "I see you got a white handkerchief tied to
your rifle. Gonna blow your nose, or is that your way of signaling
fer another free drink?"

Wade laughed. "You boys sure done a good one on me."

The man laughed heartily, and feeling confident no one else
was around, he put his pistol back in his holster. "Where's your two
friends, still trying to find the herd?" He laughed again, and this
time his weasel-like friend joined in. The other four rustlers were
now in a circle around Wade, and the cattle, without anyone to prod
them, slowed to a halt and began grazing.

"Not exactly," said Wade. "I suspect they're around here
somewhere. Probably got a bead on you right now."

The big man's laugh slowly faded as he once again took a

quick look along the hilltops around him. "Well, if your sure-shots were up there they would have shot me dead already. Any of you boys been shot dead yet?"

They all laughed at the big man's joke.

Wade chuckled along with them. "I reckon we all had a good laugh on that one. Now, maybe we can come to some agreement on my herd of cattle."

"What kind of agreement might that be?"

Wade glanced at the rise opposite him, but he did not see any signs of Custer and Pinky. Sitting in the middle of six armed men was not exactly to Wade's advantage at the moment, but in spite of that he was quite calm. "Me and my two friends don't have much respect for people stealing our cattle. That ain't polite, you know."

The big man grinned. "Polite," he said as he looked at his boys. "Who the hell heard of a polite rustler?" All his men were laughing again, and he went on. "You know what I do with little piss-ant cowboys like you? I usually skin 'em alive." He shoved his buckskin jacket aside to show a long bladed knife in his belt. "But, I'll tell you what. Today I'm going to put a .44 slug right between your eyes. Just to be polite, of course."

All his men laughed so hard, they practically fell out of their saddles. Wade swallowed hard. Custer, Pinky and the rest of the men were not yet in sight.

The big man was still laughing from his bowels. "Herb, take his rifle away from him."

"Wait a minute," said Wade before the man could grab his Winchester. "If you take my rifle, you boys are going to be so full of lead, your horses will collapse underneath you from the weight."

The big man's grin slowly disappeared. He once again looked at the hilltops about him, and then he directed two of his men. "Herb, Cal, you two ride up and take a look around."

Wade waved the handkerchief on the end of his rifle back and forth, and to his surprise his men were right on queue. "No need for that," he said. He pointed toward the ridge where Custer and Pinky now appeared with the other men. They were strung out in a line so precisely, that the sun shining blindly from behind presented their forms as nothing more than dark shadows.

"By Jesus!" said one of the men from behind Wade. "There's ten of 'em!"

The big man spun in his saddle, and now all eyes were on the ridge.

The weasel character strained his eyes. "They got rifles, Burt, every one of them!"

Those were sweet words to Wade's ears. From here there was no doubt it appeared each of the men was carrying a rifle. Of course, Wade knew they were nothing more than stripped tree limbs.

The big man stared at the group, then snarled. "They'd have to be pretty good shooters from that distance." He looked at Wade. "They're so far away we could shoot you dead, have time for a cup of coffee and make a stand long before they get to the bottom of that hill."

The man had a point, Wade thought to himself, and it didn't look like the rustlers were going to be bluffed. Wade suddenly needed a really big lie. "Well, if I was countin' on my two boys you're right, they ain't much good at shooting from afar, but Joe Purdy can hit a fly at three hundred yards. I'd say we were about three hundred yards from them, wouldn't you?"

"Joe Purdy?" said the big man. "I heard someone shot him dead some time back."

"Why don't you ride up there and tell him that? That's Joe on the left next to his two brothers."

The weasel shielded his eyes against the sun. "Damn, I think that is him!" The power of suggestion was working in Wade's favor. The other men behind Wade now started mumbling among themselves. It was obvious they all knew Joe Purdy's reputation.

Wade went on. "Joe's got one of those newfangled telescope rifles. He can see a wart on your nose from there." The rustlers still had their eyes glued on the line of horses on the hill, and it appeared they were all listening to Wade, so he kept making up more stories. "See those two little fellers on the end? They ain't even seventeen, but each one of them has killed five men. And that dog up there ain't no normal cattle dog. He's known as a killer horse dog. Half wolf and half-wild bull. You try to ride out of here without my permission and that dog will come down here and eat the leg off your horse.

"And another thing, Purdy and his bunch don't like clean killing. They'd rather gut shoot you and let you linger a couple days before you die."

The weasel had sweat on his forehead, and even the big man, as tough as he seemed to be earlier, was biting at his lip.

It was suddenly so still that everyone heard Wade cock the hammer on his rifle. "All I got to do is fire one round and you boys will be so full of holes you'll be able to hear the wind whistle through your chest."

"I'm getting out of here," said the weasel.

"Let's go, boys," said the big man.

"Not so fast!" commanded Wade feeling real brave. "I'm afraid you're going to have to leave your hardware here."

It suddenly became so quiet, as if the group of men was standing in the eye of a storm. The men behind Wade threw their pistols and rifles down, and then all the rest dropped their weapons to the ground, including the big man with the red and white polka dot shirt.

"You ain't gonna shoot us in the back, are you?" asked the big man.

Wade was cocky now. "I ain't decided yet."

The rustlers slapped their horses and rode off so fast, a lightning bolt couldn't have caught them. By the time they were over the hill, Custer, Pinky and the rest of the men came down off the ridge.

Custer and Pinky were jubilant, but the rest of the men were more concerned about their payment in cattle. As promised, Wade had them pick out their four head.

Before they left, Zeb came over to Wade. "We sure do thank you for your generosity," he said. "You kept your word, and for that we're grateful. As for them rustlers, there ain't nothing lower, cep'n snake shit in a wagon rut." He touched his hat in a polite departing gesture, turned and rode off to catch up with his men.

Wade, Custer and Pinky watched the men until they were over the hill and out of sight. For the longest time, neither of them said anything. They were all reflecting on what Zeb had said about rustlers.

"What now?" asked Custer.

"We take the herd to Abilene, sell the cattle, and turn the

money over to the bank like we ought to."

Custer made a face. "What's Mr. Russell goin' to say when he discovers we lost four head of cattle and a couple horses?"

"We lost more than four head," said Wade. "I'm guessing we lost a dozen or so during the stampede."

"Hell, we done saved his herd from rustlers!" said Pinky.

"Yeah," said Wade. "But Russell probably won't view it that way. Wouldn't surprise me if he fired us."

Pinky frowned. "What we gonna do then?"

"First thing we're going to do is sell them pistols and Winchesters we took from the rustlers."

"How much you figger that will bring?" asked Pinky.

"Two hundred, maybe two hundred fifty dollars."

"Whoowhee!"

Wade went on. "And then we're going to get a hotel room, a case of champagne, and a real hot bath." A hot bath was something the three cowboys had never had.

Pinky and Custer were grinning from ear to ear.

"We sure bluffed them rustlers, didn't we?" said Custer.

"We sure did," said Wade.

The three started swinging their lassos at the heels of the cattle. If they could get the herd up over the ridge, they would still have another hour of daylight.

* * *

LUCK OF THE DRAW

Breakfast was the usual, biscuits with watered down gravy left over from some poor quality beef a few days back. Jessup, like the rest of the crew, ate the food without complaint. He finished up and dumped his pan and silverware in the chuckwagon pot just as Ray Ford rode up on his horse. He dismounted, grabbed a cup of coffee from the pot on the fire and began calling off the positions of the day.

Ray was foreman for the XT herd. "Caleb, Barns front flankers, Spud and Jute rear flankers. Bobby, you take point with Ezrel. Jessup, you relieve Colter on the remuda so's he can get breakfast, then you and Emmet take drag.

"Yessuh," said Jessup.

Jessup had pretty much figured out the system by now. In two and a half months on the cattle trail, he had heard the same schedule almost every morning. Of course, most of the men switched from point to one of the flankers and occasionally to drag, but in the past seventy-five days, Jessup had been pulling drag four out of five days. Drag was the dirtiest position, bringing up the rear of the cattle, eating a pound of dirt a day from the clouds of dust they stirred up.

Those that lagged behind he could bring in line with the snap of his lariat, his basic chore. He always buttoned his shirt at the neck, wore a bandana over his nose and mouth, pulled his hat down as far as he could and spent most of the day squinting to keep the dust out. But nothing worked.

On a hot day—and almost all days were hot—he was a little more miserable. He had signed on because he needed work like all the rest of the cowboys. He didn't mind driving cattle, but it did not seem fair. Four out of every five days on drag.

Chow time came and Jessup hurried to the chuckwagon when it was his turn. He wolfed down the beans and salt pork, then headed for the remuda where he caught his favorite horse, Blue, a blue-black stud. He didn't' even need to rope the animal. Blue knew the routine just as well as Jessup. When Jessup rode up, Blue dropped back from the remuda and waited patiently while Jessup took the saddle and bridle off of his morning horse, Big Dog. He slapped it on Blue, mounted up and headed back for the rear of the herd.

"Come on, big boy," Jessup said to Blue as he spurred him on. "Better squint your eyes, cause today it's dustier than normal." The trail had been dry for two weeks, not even a lone drop of rain anywhere within a hundred miles.

The day passed into afternoon when Jessup changed horses again, got a drink from the chuckwagon, then was back on drag. When the sun started dipping behind the horizon, the crew let the cattle coast until they came to a near halt and started grazing. The routine for them was always the same, just like the sun always comes up in the morning, just like a prairie rose always sprouts in spring.

Several of the cowpunchers sat around the fire after their meal listening to Caleb playing lightly on a harmonica. Ray Ford stretched his long lanky legs out as he leaned on a wagon wheel, figuring in his black book like he did most evenings. Jessup never knew what he was writing for sure, probably kept count of the days on a calendar so he knew how many more days would be required to reach Kansas City. Or maybe took notes on the progress of the crew. Jessup couldn't read or write, so even if he ever saw the contents of the book, he wouldn't know what was said anyway.

Jessup was itching from the dust he had collected during the day and was not too thrilled about riding drag again tomorrow. He had signed on in Fort Worth, hired by John Davidson, the owner of the herd. Like the others, he was told he would receive equal treatment by the foreman even though he was the newest to join the outfit.

Jessup kept thinking about the book Ray Ford was now writing in. Perhaps the man kept track of who rode point, who rode flank, who rode drag. Maybe somehow, Jessup's name was not written in correctly, or if the foreman had a calendar, maybe he didn't realize Jessup was spending four out of five days riding that miserable position.

Jessup went over to Ray Ford and sat down next to him.

"Somethin' wrong?" asked Ray. His jaw hung low, and he gave that scowl he possessed when things didn't seem to be going right. Jessup thought maybe it would be better to ask on another day, but he mustered up some courage.

"Mister Ford, suh. I been ridin' drag now four out of every five days."

Ray didn't blink an eye. "So?"

"Well, I figured maybe you didn't realize that. Maybe your book there don't have me listed correctly."

"My notations are none of your business."

Caleb abruptly stopped playing his harmonica. The only sound in the night was an occasional lowing of the cattle, and all eyes were on Jessup now.

A sudden discomfort overtook Jessup, but he felt he hadn't been treated fairly. "Mister Ford, suh. I been kinda keepin' track of who's riding where, and I..."

"That's my job, not yours."

"Well, suh, I noticed Bobby never has rode drag. Most the rest of us has, but Bobby ain't never. And it seems I'm ridin' drag most every day."

"I decide who rides where," said Ray. The scowl never left his face.

"But Mr. Davidson said when I signed on, I was to..."

"Mr. Davidson put me in charge, Jessup. I'm the foreman.

You take orders from me when Mr. Davidson ain't around."

Obviously Jessup couldn't talk to Mr. Davidson, because he was in Fort Worth. "Well, it's just somethin' I want you to think about," said Jessup as he stood up.

"I will, Jessup," said Ray. "I'll stay up all night thinking about what you said." A few of the men chuckled at the snide comment.

Jessup felt uneasy, but he stood his ground. "All I'm askin' fer is a fair shake. I ain't never shirked my duty."

Ray Ford closed his book and stood up. He was as tall as Jessup, but Jessup was well built, muscled, forty or fifty pounds heavier than he was. "Jessup, I fought the damn war over you and your kind and lost three brothers. The only kin I got left is Bobby. I make the decisions who rides where and who does what. Right now, you saddle up and get your black hide out there and take night guard."

Jessup stared at the man, eyed the other men around the fire. None of them had the courage to look up. And now it was clear to Jessup why he was riding the dirtiest job on the trail drive.

The war had cost everybody something. No one had bothered to ask Jessup if he suffered any losses during the war. He lost his wife and his two young children, all burned to death by a bunch of Yankee outlaw soldiers. He had many close friends at the beginning of the war, but most of them were gone now. Of course, he now had his freedom, something he never guessed would happen during his lifetime. Being free from slavery had cost him dearly, and now, two years after the war, the price was still mounting.

When would the price go down? he was thinking as he rode out to relieve one of the night guards. It didn't make any sense. The North who fought to free him was responsible for wiping out his family, and Ray, who fought for the South, seemed to be blaming the loss of his family on him and his kind. Jessup, himself, had fought with the Confederates at Menassas, a bloody battle. That's where he had learned to shoot, but nobody knew that either.

In the morning, Ray handed out the assignments again. "Spud

and Jute, front flankers, Caleb and Barns take rear flankers. Bobby, you take point with Emmet. Jessup, you relieve Colter on the remuda so's he can get breakfast, then you and Ezrel take drag."

Yes, Jessup had the system down, and it didn't look like it was going to change much, at least, not for him.

A few days later, they crossed the Canadian and kept skirting the eastern edge of Oklahoma Territory. That dip in the water had been refreshing, but now they were on the trail for four more hot days in a row.

In the afternoon Jessup traded horses at the remuda and saddled up Blue once again. He rode to the chuckwagon for some water where Emmet was getting a drink. Ambrose, the chuckwagon cook, was sitting in the shade of the wagon resting his old bones, sweating heavily, his face the color of a red rooster.

"Sho is a hot one," said Jessup as he dipped a ladle into the barrel.

"Sure is," said Emmet. He wiped his brow with his bandana and puffed out his cheeks. "How the hell much more of this can we take?"

He never got an answer. A thumping sound struck Emmet directly in the chest and knocked him down. A spurt of blood leaked out where a bullet struck him. More shots sounded and bullets tore up the grass around Jessup. He whipped around, spotted them on a rise two hundred yards away.

"Rustlers!" he shouted.

Ambrose scrambled for the seat of his wagon, snapped the reins and tore off.

Jessup had no gun, but Emmet did. He pulled the Winchester from the scabbard on Emmet's horse, jumped on Blue and spurred him as hard as he could.

The cattle were on the run now, their horns clicking ferociously against each other, the pounding hooves a threatening, punishing sound on the prairie. Jessup heard more shots, saw two riders swing in his direction. From the other side of the herd, three more riders came riding hard.

"Oh, my Lord!" he said to himself. He pressed his horse on, heading his horse for a cache of trees. Once behind them, he jerked his horse to a halt. In a few seconds one of the rustler's rode by. Jessup knocked him out of the saddle in one shot.

The second rider was right behind him. He had a revolver and fired at Jessup, but a pistol at his range and at that speed was useless. Jessup took careful aim and dropped him out of the saddle.

Jessup kicked his horse again and ran along with the cattle. The three riders on the other side of the running herd were after Barns and Spud. Neither of the XT hands were good shots with a rifle even though both had Winchesters. Jessup gave his horse full rein, twisting in his saddle looking for more rustlers.

Ahead in the middle of the herd he saw Bobby picking his way through the swirling dust, trying to reach this side of the stampeding cattle. Jessup urged his horse some more. A shot rang out and Bobby's horse went down. Immediately Jessup swung into the herd and raced for him. Bobby was on his feet, and as Jessup charged in, Bobby grabbed an arm. Jessup pulled him up behind and sped on, making his way to the outside of the herd.

A set of low hills kept the cattle to a narrow pathway and in seconds Jessup made it to safety. He dropped Bobby off and turned in time to see two more riders coming hard at him. He fired a shot, missed his first one, fired again and saw the man fall from his horse into the path of the pounding hooves.

The second rider turned and rode back through the cattle to the far side. Jessup rode on some more. A shot rang out from across the herd and Jessup saw another rustler tumble from his horse. Ray had picked him off.

There were a few more riders on the far side, but suddenly they headed up over a rise out of sight. Jessup pulled his horse to a halt, could see Ray across from him. Some of the other hands had ridden on ahead, chasing after Ambrose in the chuckwagon.

It seemed the rustlers had given up, and Jessup smiled triumphantly. It was then a bullet struck him in the back and he flopped over his saddle. The Winchester dropped from his hand and a moment later he slipped off Blue to the ground. The last sounds he heard were two gunshots as he lay flat, his eyes staring into the blue sky.

A half-hour later, Ray Ford and the rest of the crew stood over Jessup's body. The only other hand who had died besides Jessup was Emmet, killed with the first shot.

Ray Ford's haggard face stared down at Jessup. "There were nine of them, I figure," he said. "We got five. We were lucky."

Tears welled up in Bobby's eyes as he looked at Jessup. "He got three of them, Ray. Jessup shot three hisself."

Ray seemed stunned. He looked over the faces of the remaining men. None of them had killed anyone, and Ray knew he killed the other two.

"He saved my life, Ray," said Bobby. "Jessup picked me up when they shot my horse out from under me. He didn't have to ride into that mess, but he did."

Ray nodded. "The man never did shirk his duty, did he?" He eyed each of the men. Their faces were solemn, their silence as rare as a night without coyotes.

"Bring Emmet up here and let's give these boys a proper burial."

They buried the two men that afternoon on a high rise and made two markers. No one said a prayer, but the absence of words still gave the procedure a sense of resolution.

By nightfall they had rounded up the cattle, and by Ray's count only twelve were missing.

That night around the campfire was the quietest evening anyone could remember. The pleasant sounds of Caleb's harmonica seemed to take the place of normal conversation.

In the morning, Ray Ford gave the usual orders and mounted his horse. You boys keep the herd moving north. I need to find some extra hands."

Four hours later in late morning he arrived in Tahlequa. The town wasn't much more than a few scattered buildings, most lined up north to south. The courthouse, a large brick building standing off by itself, was the most prominent structure. A few young trees were springing up here and there. Other than that, the town lay in a flat, peaceful valley surrounded by low hills.

This was an Indian town, Cherokees, Ray knew, one of the five civilized tribes. He also knew they had a newspaper office, which he located in short time. He had the owner print up a half dozen posters that announced anyone looking for work should show up at the general store at two in the afternoon. He posted the announcements in various places, then found the sheriff's office and reported where the five dead rustlers could be found. There wasn't much the sheriff could do other than send out a wagon to pick them up, and Ray guessed as much. He had lunch and a cold beer in a hotel restaurant and then waited on the boardwalk in front of the general store to see if there were any takers.

Near two in the afternoon, they began to drift in, and on the hour there were eight men seeking work. Four were Indians, two were white, two were black. Not a one of them looked remotely like a cowpuncher, and when Ray questioned them, only two admitted to having some savvy about cattle. They all claimed they could ride a horse, but Ray even had his doubts about that.

"Gentlemen," he addressed the ragged looking men. "I need two men to help push a herd to Kansas City. Any objections to that?"

No one had any.

"I'm going to be impartial about my decision. Everybody sign your name on a piece of paper and we'll draw two names out of my hat. If you can't write, I'll write your name for you. Fair enough?"

They all agreed.

Only four could write. Ray wrote the rest of their names for them and mixed the slips up in his hat. "And so's this drawing is fair, I've asked this young boy to do the picking." A freckle-faced youngster, who had been watching all along, gave a healthy smile.

"Pick me, Billy!" someone hollered from the group. Some laughter came with the comment from the men and the small crowd of onlookers that had gathered.

The boy reached in the hat, pulled a name and read it out loud. "Amos."

Amos was one of the black men. He stepped forward with a happy look on his face.

The youngster pulled another name. "Jaspar."

The other black man stepped forward.

Ray looked at the two men, looked back at the rest of the men. "Thank you, gentlemen."

A few of the men grumbled as they dispersed, and the rest of the onlookers slowly drifted away. Ray scrutinized the appearance of the two black men before him. They had bedrolls and wore beat up hats. Their clothes were tattered and worn and looked as if they would blow off in a stiff wind.

"You boys come with me." He led them inside the general store and instructed the owner to give each of the men a set of clothes, complete with underwear and socks. "Pick yourselves out a hat and a good pair of boots and spurs. If you two are going to push cattle, you might as well at least look like cowboys."

"Yessuh," they both said in unison.

"When you're dressed come on down to the livery. I'll have a couple horses picked out for you."

After Ray left the general store, the owner looked at the two black men and said, "You must be the two fellows what got picked."

"Yessuh, said Amos. "We done got the luck of the draw."

An hour later Ray and the two black cowboys rode down the main street of Tahlequa, planning on reaching the herd before nightfall.

As they passed the general store, the young freckle-faced boy gave a wave.

His mother came up behind him. "Where did you get that sack of candy sticks?" she asked.

"From that man," he said as he pointed to Ray Ford. "All I had to do was pick two names out of a hat and read 'em off."

"Billy, you can't read."

"Didn't need to, mom. He said no matter what name came up, I was to say Amos and Jasper."

The young boy waved again. Ray touched the brim of his hat and gave a broad smile. Moments later, he and the two lucky cowboys had turned the corner and were out of sight.

* * *

THE SECRET OF THE TRIBES

Spotted Elk lay on the low banks of the river, his head bent over the edge until the top of his head touched the water. He flopped his long hair forward and leaned down even farther, letting the flowing water rinse his hair. The water was warm today on this warm morning, but refreshing. Later in the day Spotted Elk would bathe here when the sun was three quarters across the sky, the hottest part of the day.

He sat on the bank now, his legs crossed as his wife ran a comb through his hair. When it was dry she began putting it back into the braids Spotted Elk preferred, her hands soft and gentle, as they always were.

Four younger children ran past with sticks driving hoops along the bank, their cries of excitement witnessed by those near by. And there were many, among them the Sans Arc, the Arapahos, the Cheyenne and Hunkpapa Sioux. Other tribes were at the north end of this grand gathering, all brought together because of the times. Spotted Elk remembered a time when twenty of his braves could easily defend themselves against an equal number of the white warriors. But the times had changed. For every brave lost in battle, a younger one was in line to take his place. But for every white soldier killed it seemed five more were sent to take his place.

For Spotted Elk these numbers were staggering. He had no idea where they all came from. He only knew that they were pushing the tribes further west with each passing of the full moon. There was a time many years past when his tribe used to inherit the land among the big lakes of the north, five of them so his Great Grandfather had told him. Spotted Elk had no idea where those five big lakes were located. There were many times he wished he could visit such vast bodies of water, but sadly, he did not think that would happen during his lifetime.

"What are you thinking, husband?" his wife asked.

"I was thinking about the great lakes my Great Grandfather told me about."

"And you would like to see them someday, but that day will never come," she added.

She knew him well, seemed to know many of his thoughts before he even thought of them, he mused.

"Are you watching out for our children?" he asked.

"No need to," she answered. "Our children are the most wonderful of all the tribes. They can take care of themselves."

He gave her a stern look.

She laughed. "Young Elk and Two Feathers are with their uncle. Princess is visiting a friend. Of course I know where the children are."

She was a good woman for Spotted Elk, and he knew it. She was his third wife. The first two had been killed by the white soldiers along with three of his children. Spotted Elk had every reason to be bitter on this hot summer morning, but he chose not to today. He simply wanted to enjoy the gurgling of the shallow stream before him, the hot wind that rustled the leaves of the tree above, the splendor of the wind-swept grass knolls all around the valley. These earthly wonders existed because of the Great Spirit. No other power or magic could deliver such serenity, not even the medicine men in his tribe, and they had strong medicine.

Today, thought Spotted Elk, would be a day to remember. He had that feeling that comes in the form of a premonition. By the end of the day he would know if he were right or wrong.

In the afternoon Spotted Elk sat in the shade with some of

his friends, a blanket in front them, throwing dice. His horse needed grooming and there were other chores to do, but Spotted Elk and his comrades shared the same thoughts; too hot to do anything but wile away the day doing nothing.

Then, out of the lazy day came shouts in the distance. The men looked up from their game as a crier at the far end of the camp galloped in their direction. He was shouting as he rode, pointing behind him.

"Soldiers!" they finally heard him say. They were on their feet immediately and ran to the path where the Indian was approaching. He slowed enough to holler at them, "Soldiers! Many soldiers at the south bend of the river! Soldiers!" He urged his horse on, crying the word as he went.

Spotted Elk and his friends ran for their teepees. Everywhere to the south of them braves were mounting their horses, rifles in hand, racing toward the far end of the camp.

Now, Spotted Elk could hear the gunfire, recognized easily the reports of the white man's carbine. There were many shots, too many to count as he grabbed the repeater rifle from his tent. His horse was grazing several hundred yards away. He ran as fast as he could, other neighbors now alongside him, racing in the same direction. Spotted Elk cursed as he caught his horse and swung up on his back. He had had no time to put on his war paint or decorate his horse. He hoped the Great Spirit would forgive him for this unprepared entry into battle. He kicked his horse in the flanks and joined the many braves now riding along with him.

As he raced through the camp, women and children were scurrying in all directions, their shouts and screams full of alarm for such a beautiful day.

Oh, Great Spirit, Spotted Elk thought to himself, *give me the courage of the mountain lion and the strength of the buffalo. Let me be among the leaders and guide me into battle as you have guided no other warrior.*

His thoughts shifted from the spiritual as he saw the line of horsemen approaching. He made a quick count, thinking there must be thousands of them, but even now as he neared, there were not nearly that many, and several had dismounted, now firing from the ground. Almost immediately they were mounting their horses again, ready for an attack.

But no, now they turned and ran back toward the river. Was this some sort of diversion? Was there a bigger force in the trees near the river? Spotted Elk raised his rifle and fired, worked the action on the repeater and fired again. He looked around him, could see many of his comrades chasing after the soldiers.

The battle ensued, and Spotted Elk had fired many rounds of his rifle, advancing, it seemed, after each round.

He could hear shots from all around him, could hear yells and commands of the white man's tongue, none of it at all understandable. Dust swirled in every direction, soldiers lay crumpled on the ground. Those that were slightly wounded met their end as braves hacked at them with stone mallets, shot them at close range. This was not a time to stop for scalps, since the soldiers were retreating, leaping their horses into the water, forcing their horses to climb impossible banks on the other side.

Horses and riders tumbled backwards into the water. Bullets from his people found their mark. Where a soldier fell in the water, red flowed with the current, his blood life draining away.

How much time passed, Spotted Elk did not know. He heard his name called out. Two Bears, an arrow's distance away was shouting, pointing to the east. Spotted Elk saw the swells of dust on the horizon and knew there were more soldiers.

"Come!" he heard Two Bears shout again.

Spotted Elk gave his horse rein, and as he caught up to Two Bears, other braves were joining him. Now there were five braves, driving their horses back to camp at full force, pressing their animals savagely.

They reached the edge of their camp and sped their horses through the tents, shouting for their people to get out of the way. To their right, on the hill, they saw the line of troopers strung out on their gray mounts, all headed in the same direction they were headed.

Spotted Elk feared the worst. He was sure the attack he had just encountered was in some measure a diversion. Why else would such a force attack and then pull back?

The camp was in a frenzy, women hurrying seemingly in all directions seeking their children, older warriors standing guard by their lodges with lances and bows, ready to defend their families at all costs.

Spotted Elk looked behind him. It appeared all Indian braves were fighting near the river. Very few braves were at this end of the camp, and this is where more blue coats were headed.

"Here! Here!" shouted Two Bears as he reined in his horse. The five all tugged their horses to a halt and focused their eyes on the bluff across the river. The blue coats were now coming down the slope, attacking the middle of the camp.

How strange, Spotted Elk was thinking. There were not thousands of men as he suspected, but a small force, maybe two hundred men. Were they brave or foolish? he kept asking himself.

The five Indians jumped from their horses and ran for cover near the river. They crouched behind a bank, all armed with repeating rifles, all shoving cartridges into the magazines of their weapons. Poised and patient, they waited, watched as the column of men rushed at the river. A bugle sounded as they neared, a lead trooper held a steady course, a lance poked upward from his stirrup with a flag waving at the peak.

The hooves of the oncoming horses thundered like a heard of buffalo. The sound was deafening, threatening, the riders coming ever closer.

In the lead was a man with a tan jacket and breeches. His pistol was drawn and he was shouting at his men, urging them on, giving confidence at every moment.

As they neared the river, Spotted Elk knew his course. "The one in the buckskin jacket!" he shouted at the braves next to him.

"The one in the lead, everyone take aim at him. Everyone! Wait until they enter the water. Wait! Wait!"

Two Bears, Crazy Wolf, Four Fingers, Kills The Enemy and Spotted Elk all had their rifles pointed, hammers back, their aim sure.

As soon as the first onslaught of soldiers reached the water, Spotted Elk gave the command to fire.

The barrage of five rifles ripped across the short distance of the river and struck the man in the buckskin jacket. He flipped backward off his horse into the water, his pistol flying in the air.

The line of soldiers halted, their shouts now a call of despair. Two soldiers quickly dismounted, grabbed for the man in buckskin. More shots poured at the soldiers. One of the helpers went down, another took his place. The five braves fired time after time, making their marks. Bullets now came back at them, tufts of dirt spewing up in front of them.

Along the river, more braves came running on their horses. Some stopped and joined the five, others went on ahead and found positions along the bank. In short time hundreds of braves were now lining the river, and with commands from the great Oglala warrior, Crazy Horse, several warriors charged across the river. "Hoka-hey!" he shouted. "Brave hearts follow me!"

The soldiers were now in retreat running back up the hill from where they had come. Some soldiers left the main column looking for cover in nearby ravines. Warriors pursued them, shooting them down as if in a buffalo chase.

Lame Deer, another great chief, hollered for warriors to follow him. With a huge number of men, he ran up the hillside, flanking the soldiers who had reached the hilltop. The gunfire was incessant. Occasionally a brave was shot from his horse, but now the soldiers had dismounted and were making a stand, taking their toll.

Spotted Elk and the men with him sprang for their horses and raced across the river, pushed them at all speed up the hill. The gunfire was deafening, shouts of encouragement screamed from the lungs of the charging Indians.

In the time it requires to eat a meal, the gunfire had practically stopped. The blue coats were strewn along the hillside, most of them at the top, all dead or dying, almost every horse down or dying.

Gunshots could be heard from three miles away, a skirmish still going on at the south end of the camp. But here, on this hilltop, the fighting had come to an end. All the soldiers were down, scalping was in progress, mutilation of bodies left blood soaking up the soil.

Spotted Elk found the man in the canvas pants, his jacket gone, his blue shirtfront spattered with blood. The other four who had also fired at this man in the river were at his side.

"Who is he?" asked one of the men.

"He is known as Hi-estzie among the Cheyenne," said Spotted Elk.

"The Lakota call him Pe-hin Hanska," said Two Bears.

The different tribes had various names for Long Hair, and all had heard of General Custer, the great Indian fighter.

The men stared at the soldier, his dead face as calm and complacent as if he were sleeping.

"We killed him!" exclaimed one of the braves.

"Yes, we killed Long Hair!" said another.

"No!" said Spotted Elk. "None of us killed him. If it is known who killed him, the white men will seek us out. If it was a Cheyenne, they will kill all the Cheyenne. If it was a Sioux, they will kill all the Sioux. No. This is a secret we must keep, a secret of the tribes. Is it agreed?"

The men were silent, their gazes fixed on the great Indian fighter.

Two Bears was the first to speak. "Yes, it is agreed."

The rest nodded their heads.

Spotted Elk looked across the valley of the Big Horn. Distant gunfire was muffled, but constant.

"Come," said Spotted Elk. "There is more fighting to be done."

The five warriors, the killers of Custer, leaped on their horses shouting cries of victory as they headed back along the ridge.

* * *

Author's note: Most historians agree Custer never approached the Little Bighorn River, but some eyewitnesses at the battle say he did, and some say Custer was the first to fall among his troops. None of us know for certain which version is the correct one, and that is the beauty of historical fiction.

STARA KOCHKA

Katerina finished cutting up the vegetables, placed them in the iron kettle, then hung the kettle over the fire. She wiped her hands and went outdoors. Little Josephine and Joseph were playing not far behind the farmhouse in a small grove of trees. She could hear their yelps and cries of fun.

Emil, her husband, and John, the eldest son, were in the field working. She was about to return inside when she saw the wagon appear on the road. It was her neighbor, Georg Shashek. He normally passed about this time each evening after spending a day in the city selling vegetables.

"Evening," Georg offered as he pulled his horse drawn wagon to a halt. "I stopped at the post office. There was a letter for you. From America," he added, as he passed it over.

Katerina's big eyes got bigger. "America? It must be from Johan and Hilda Wagner." She turned the envelope over. "Yankton, Dakota Territory. Do you know where that is?" she asked Georg.

Georg blew out a huge puff of smoke from his pipe. " I don't quite know where America is." Georg was up in his years. "I hope it's good news," he said as he flipped his reins to get his horse moving. "See you in the morning."

Katerina quickly read the letter, and when she finished, she glanced at the sun. Emil would be working another hour yet.

After dinner, the children played or read, and when they were in bed, Katerina produced the letter from her apron and placed it on the table before Emil. He had no sooner read the letter, when Katerina laid a map on the table and placed a finger on a spot. "That must be the place," she said.

Emil studied the map. He could not read English, but Dakota Territory was clearly marked on the map, as was Yankton, one of the very few cities listed.

"They have plenty of land, Emil," remarked Katerina excitedly.

"We have our own land here," he retorted.

"Forty acres," said Katerina. "Johan and Hilda have four times that amount. And after five years it's theirs, free."

"That can't be," said Emil.

"It's the law, Emil."

"No one gets free land," said Emil.

"Read the letter, Emil!" Katerina snapped back. "This is a new, big land. This is our opportunity, don't you see that?"

"We don't speak English. How will we get along?"

"We will learn English. Johan and Hilda said they live in a Czech community. All the farmers speak Czech there. And they're all learning English. We can too."

"We'd have to sell everything here, the farm, the equipment. My father farmed this piece of land all his life, and his father before him, and..."

"Emil! My god, you're as much a slave to this land as your father was. Are we any better off now than we were fifteen years ago?" She waited for an answer. "Well, are we?"

Emil folded his hands and looked down at the table. They had had this discussion many times before.

"Johan and Hilda Wagner have been there over a year and a half now. They told us to come. They will sponsor us. They will give us a place to live until we can make arrangements for the land."

Emil simply looked at his folded hands, and after awhile he said, "We will talk about this in the morning."

Katerina tossed her hands up in the air. "My god, Emil, don't you have any courage? Can't you see that we have nothing here? Can't you..."

"We will talk about this in the morning!" he barked. He went to the bedroom and slammed the door.

Katerina sat at the table and draped her head in her hands. When she was sixteen years old Katerina married Emil. There were many times in the past few years when she questioned why she had married him. He came from a good family, and he was basically a good husband and father. But life here on the outskirts of Prague was hard. The acreage was small, taxes were large. It was simple for Katerina. The reason to immigrate to America was for the opportunity to gain free land and a better life. A much better life. Why couldn't her husband see that?

The restrictions in Czechoslovakia had been lifted a few years ago, and many Czechs were migrating to the new land of America. Katerina had implored Emil to sell the property two years ago, but he was obstinate.

"Bullheaded!" she blurted out.

In the morning Katerina prepared breakfast, and Emil ate it silently like he always did and then left for the field. He did not mention anything more about going to America.

Life continued its tedious pace for her. Over the course of the next year a few more letters arrived from the Wagners. They were so encouraging, that each time Katerina read them, she cried, but never in the presence of Emil.

One hot afternoon, John came running back to the house. "Mama, mama! Come quick! It's papa!"

She ran after John into the field, and there lay Emil on his back, his eyes wide open, perspiration still heavy on his face. The reins of the horse were still draped around his shoulders. Katerina slowly sank to her knees in the dirt and looked at her husband's dead stare.

"Is he going to be okay, mama?" she remembered John saying.

Then she heard the other two children come running up from behind her.

Two days later Emil was buried on the hill where his father was buried and where his grandfather was buried along with countless other relatives that stretched back a hundred years.

Emil Dvorak was only thirty-six years old when he died.

Neighbors helped put in the crop that summer and the same neighbors helped harvest it.

During this time, Katerina sought out a lawyer in Prague by the name of Frank Chalupnik. He was recommended by some of her friends, and was a man who handled legal matters dealing with real estate.

"I think I have a buyer for your farm," Frank Chalupnik told her one fall afternoon. He had traveled out to the farm on his horse on this and many other occasions. She had seen him as many times in the city. In fact, over a three-month period, people began to talk about the two. Rumor came to Katerina through friends, that she and Mr. Chalupnik were having an affair. Even Emil's brother brought up the subject and asked outright whether the rumors were true or not.

"And what if they are?" Katerina said firmly standing her ground. "It's none of your business."

After all, Mr. Chalupnik was a single man, never had married. But the time lapse between Emil's death and the so-called affair with Frank Chalupnik was a disgrace to Emil's side of the family.

Emil's relatives were taken aback when suddenly in December of the same year, Katerina Dvorak and Frank Chalupnik were married.

But the gossip didn't stop there. In March of the next year, the farmstead was sold, and unannounced to any of the relatives, Katerina and Frank Chalupnik left for Bremen, Germany, the port of embarkation, along with the three children, John, Joseph and Josephine.

Their ship left in late February for the journey across the ocean, which would require sixteen to eighteen days they were told. Having Frank Chalupnik for a husband had proved to be invaluable. As a lawyer, he had friends in a variety of places, and he had connections. Arranging for passage had been mostly his doing, but of course always with the prodding of Katerina.

The quarters on board ship were cramped, and the facilities for cleaning oneself and performing bodily functions had erased any sense of privacy. In spite of the inconveniences, the first few days were full of excitement. Daily conversations centered on this city called New York, a port where all immigrants had to report before being admitted to America.

But one week out of port, the days were fraught with heavy seas and a dampness that invaded even the heartiest flesh. Seasickness began to take its toll. Those who were lucky enough managed to vomit over the side, but some children and older sick people were less fortunate. Soon the smell of vomit seemed to encompass every compartment, every breath of air. Baggage for all was at a minimum, as well as medicine, and diarrhea was rampant. The journey was undertaken without a ship's doctor, thus remedies for recovery came from the minds and hands of anyone on board who had the slightest expertise for solving illnesses of any sort.

Though conditions were far from ideal, children seemed to endure the monotony better than the adults. They played a variety of games whenever possible, since toys were not among the essentials for such a trip.

Frank was one of the adults who took ill. At first his sickness was diagnosed as simple seasickness, but soon he developed a severe cough. In a short three days, pneumonia set in, and on March 11, 1871, Frank Chalupnik was buried at sea.

He was the only member of the crew and families on board who died during the trip. Katerina had been at his side almost every moment up until the last breath. It was a short ceremony, and although dropping a body into the ocean seemed inhuman for a burial, there was not much else one could do with a cadaver at sea. The captain of the ship had performed many such burials, and he assured Katerina, that such an undertaking on board ship was an honorable sendoff into the heavens.

Surprisingly, the children did not cry during the ceremony, and neither did Katerina.

* * *

When the ship reached New York, all of the migrating families were ushered into a huge building, where the height of excitement permeated the air. But soon, the immigrants were assigned to areas where they must wait their turn, and once again monotony set it. It was understandable. Hundreds of other families had arrived on a multitude of ships from every foreign country imaginable, and processing was slow, since many of the officials who filled out the questionnaires could not speak foreign languages. They seemed to rely on immigrants who had at least some command of the English language to help them out.

One of these immigrant helpers was a young man named Roman Tupa. Katerina had met him briefly on board ship, but did not realize he spoke English. He was in his early twenties, she guessed, at least ten years younger than she was.

During one of the many lulls in processing, Katerina learned that the young man was from the same province she had come from. The nearness of their home places led to cheerful conversation.

When Katerina's turn came with the officials, Roman Tupa was asked to interpret for her. During the questioning, a doctor was summoned to examine Josephine's eye, which was extremely sore and red. He directed a question at the interpreter and Roman translated for Katerina.

"He asks how long your daughter's eye has been infected," said Roman.

"For the better part of a week," answered Katerina.

Roman clarified in Czech, which the officials did not understand. "They rejected a woman earlier for a similar sore eye. They said the woman had a contagious disease."

Katerina kept her composure. "What... shall I tell them?"

"I will handle it," Roman said.

Roman spoke to the official, then to the doctor who looked at Josephine for a few seconds, and then gave a nod.

The official stamped the papers and motioned for Katerina and the children to move on to the next station. When she looked at the papers she noticed they had written in her former name, Dvorak. She didn't know why, but it was as if Frank Chalupnik, her second husband, never existed.

"What did you tell them?" Katerina asked.

"I said she was playing with the other children and got hit in the eye with a stick."

"Thank you," said Katerina. She knew that if Josephine was rejected, the entire family would have had to return to Czechoslovakia, for she most certainly would not have abandoned her daughter. "I must get a poultice for her eye when we get out of here." She sighed. The line at the next station was as long as the line she had just waited in.

Toward evening, Katerina finally was passed through immigration. Roman was a gentleman and proved very useful. It so happened he too was headed for Chicago by train, and so Katerina and the children spent the next four days in his company. Daily, Katerina prepared a milk poultice for Josephine's eye, and by the time they reached Chicago, her eye already was improving.

In Chicago, Katerina and the children stayed in a hotel overnight since the train schedule held them up until the next day. When the children were asleep, Katerina left the room and met Roman, who was staying in the same hotel in the downstairs lobby. That evening the two strolled along the boardwalk, admiring Lake Michigan. It was late when they returned to the hotel, and it was much later when Katerina finally returned to her own room.

Another two-day trip brought Katerina and her three children to Yankton, Dakota Territory, and the end of the rail line.

Katerina knew that Johan and Hilda Wagner lived about twenty miles west along the Missouri River, but there was no stagecoach out of Yankton. She had no trouble communicating in this frontier town, since a number of people were of Czech decent.

Thus Katerina managed to find a man who was hauling a load of freight in that direction, and he offered to take Katerina and the children along. The trip required the better part of a day on a road that appeared to be fairly well traveled. Katerina, feeling so close to her destination, enjoyed every minute of the fresh, spring day. High bluffs overlooked the Missouri to the south, and as they drove further westward, the trail angled off to the north away from the river through rolling hills. It seemed that from the top of every rise, she could see a small farm, sometimes within a mile of the road, sometimes more. This was a vast, open country, and as the wagon continued on its slow journey, she had ample time to reflect. She had some money left, but hardly enough to purchase equipment to begin farming. She would need a home. Schooling for her kids was essential.

"Sir," she inquired of the driver, who also was a Czech immigrant. "How does one go about acquiring land?"

"You're talking about farming, ma'am," he asked?

"Yes."

The man thought a moment. "Which county do you intend to live in?"

"I am told Bon Homme."

"You need to apply at the courthouse in Yankton." He hesitated. "But when you join your husband, you will discover he already filed."

"I intend to file," she answered.

He looked at her for some time. "You came all this way by yourself? Is your husband joining you later?"

"My husband died on board ship."

The driver shrugged, raised his eyebrows. "My, you are a brave lady to make this trip alone."

"I'm not alone. I have my children."

The driver nodded politely, did not remark about her naiveté. Without a husband to work the land, it would be more difficult for her to file for a land grant. The rules were strict about women owning land, especially immigrant women, but this information he did not impart to her.

He halted the wagon at the bottom of a long hill where the road split. "I am going on," he told her. He pointed to the road, which lead north. "Follow this road three miles and you will come to the small town of Tabor. Outside of town there will be a white house on your left. The people who live there speak Czech and they will help you locate your friends."

Katerina thanked the man and watched him drive off. It was near four o'clock, she judged by the sun. This was the last day of April, and though the sun had been warm for most of the day, the air was now starting to cool down. She wrapped her shawl about her shoulders, picked up her bags and put on a big smile for her children. By the time they reached the small white house outside of Tabor, they were exhausted.

* * *

Katerina eventually located the Wagners, who lived a few miles outside of the small town of Tabor. The Wagners learned of the death of Emil Dvorak, and were equally surprised to discover she had remarried and lost a second husband on board ship. It was agreed that Katerina's family could remain at the Wagner farm until Katerina determined exactly what she could do to support herself. John, now 15 years of age, would help with the farm work, and Katerina would help with the household chores. The two younger children settled in quite easily to their new farm life, and spent most of the summer playing with the Wagner's children. They were given farm chores to do, but their responsibilities beyond simply being children did not amount to much more.

By the end of the summer, John and the two youngsters had gained a very good command of the English language. Katerina made an effort to study English daily with Hilda giving her support, but it was more difficult for her.

The summer seemed extremely long. Katerina had inquired whether she could apply for a land grant, and had made two trips to Yankton in the early part of the summer, expressly to talk to the officials in the courthouse about the process. But, being a woman, she did not qualify, and John would not be eligible for at least another three years. The only benefit she received from the two trips was that she met a man by the name of Albert Hrushka, a clerk in the court system. Albert was a bachelor of forty years, a few years her senior, but he had become immediately enthralled with Katerina. On her second visit, he had made it a point of renting a carriage and taking her on a picnic below the bluffs along the bottomland by the Missouri. He was most enamored on that outing, and Katerina was very receptive to his advances.

She met him four more times during late summer and early fall. The winter was long and cold, and though the two were no more than thirty miles apart, the only contact Katerina had with Albert was through correspondence.

The letter writing was, for all practical purposes, Albert's means of courting, and in April of the following year, she received a most challenging letter.

She was in the kitchen with Hilda when she finished reading the letter.

"Something new?" Hilda asked Katerina.

She looked up, beaming. "Albert said next time we meet, he has something special to ask me."

Hilda rolled her eyes. "Oh, what do you suppose that could be?" Of course she knew.

"He wants to marry me," Katerina said.

"Do you think he would be good for you," Hilda asked.

"Good for me and the children. He hasn't met the kids, but I know he will like them. He's a good man, he works hard, and he has put away some money." She paused. "And I think I could live in the city. At least I'm willing to give it a try."

Katerina made arrangements for a trip to Yankton with a neighbor who was going for supplies. When she arrived in town, she realized it was the last day of April, exactly one year from the day she had arrived in Yankton. She was excited, even giddy as she walked up the stairs of the courthouse. She had written to Albert two weeks ago that she would arrive on this day. He would, of course, be expecting her, she was sure. Otherwise he would have written back.

Once inside, she immediately walked up the staircase to the second floor to Albert's office. She did not bother to knock, simply threw the door open and looked across to Albert's desk.

Albert was not there, but a young lady, an assistant in the office, recognized her. She got up from her desk and summoned a gentleman from another room.

He was a robust man, dressed neatly in a dark suit. "You are Miss Dvorak?" he asked in Czech. She nodded and he invited her into his office and asked her to sit down.

As calmly and as politely as he could, he informed her that Albert Hrushka had taken ill four days ago and died in the hospital of a burst appendix. He had been buried the day before.

"I am very sorry," the man offered. "I know that you...had some ties with Albert."

Katerina simply stared across the room. "Not any more."

That afternoon Katerina checked into the Gurney Hotel, and having procured a bottle of whiskey through a cleaning lady who worked there, she quietly drank herself into a stupor that lasted for three days.

She did not have enough money to pay for three nights, and when she tried to leave the premises early on the fourth morning, the hotel manager caught her and had her arrested.

That day she spent in the county jail. The jailer had the decency not to lock her up, but allowed her to utilize a sitting room if she promised not to try to escape, which she did since she had not made arrangements to return to Tabor. He also provided her with hot coffee and food, for which she was very thankful.

The next morning she woke to discover she had been released. "The county judge paid your fine," said the jailer. "He said if you were looking for work, you should see him at the courthouse."

Katerina found the offer intriguing. She knew her family was all right for the moment. She cleaned herself up as best as she could and walked six blocks back to the courthouse where Albert had worked.

She met Judge Edward Koletzkij, who said he knew Albert very well and respected him, and he said he understood how terribly distraught she must have been to discover he had suddenly died.

"If you are in need and are so inclined, I have an invalid wife at my home who requires daily care. I will pay you a fair wage if you are interested."

It was a simple enough offer, and she accepted at first, simply to earn a few dollars to pay the Judge back for the compassion he had showed her by paying her fine and releasing her.

But after a week, she found a newfound respect within herself. She had not earned any money living at the Wagner's farm, and she indicated by letter that she would remain in Yankton for awhile if the children could continue living with them until she established herself well enough to send for them.

That was agreed upon. The relationship with Judge Koletzkij took a beneficial turn for Katerina. The Judge knew of a post, which would soon open up at the Greenwood Agency, some fifty miles west of Yankton along the Missouri River. The agency was where the Sioux Indians had been relocated. The job would encompass teaching the Indians how to use farm machinery, tending cattle and raising horses.

It was a generous offer, and Katerina advised John, her eldest, to apply for the job, which he did. He had to walk twenty-five miles for the interview, but word from the Judge had precluded his arrival, so when he reported in at the agency he was immediately hired on. Between John and Katerina, they could now send a few dollars a month to the Wagners for caring for the two younger children.

Katerina continued to work for the Judge as a live-in maid and nurse for his invalid wife. Over the course of the next three years, she managed to accumulate a few dollars, and every two or three months she would try to see her children at the Wagner farm or else send for them. When John was eighteen, Judge Koletzkij helped Katerina make an application for him to begin farming some land he had earmarked near Avon, a town not too distant from the agency. When John began farming, Joseph took over the job at the agency.

Judge Koletzkij's wife died less than two years later, and although Katerina's duties as a nurse had come to a halt, the Judge kept her on as a maid. He was sixty at this time and Katerina was thirty-four years old. Innuendoes were made about the relationship between the Judge and Katerina. Nothing was said when the Judge, years earlier, had helped John Dvorak procure land in Avon, but when it was deemed necessary for Katerina to travel, the Judge made all arrangements and picked up all costs. That caused some gossip to spread about town. Then, quite regularly, Katerina and the Judge began frequenting the theater. It became very clear to nearly everyone, that Katerina's role of simple maid in the household and been expanded considerably. By now, she was often referred to privately as *Stara Kochka* in the Czech language, which loosely translated meant *the old cat*.

On July 4, 1876, exactly 100 years after the Declaration of Independence, Katerina gained her citizenship. Edward Koletzkij was conspicuously present with her on this particular day. The regular Circuit Judge who normally presided over such events was out of town, and she was sworn in by a military officer who had authority to do so. This man was General Phil Sheridan, a highly respected Army officer who had been commissioned by the President of the United States to bring order to the settlement of the Indian problem in the West. At this ceremony, five years and three months after her arrival, Katerina along with four other individuals became an American. Although speaking English was not among the criteria for becoming a citizen, her fluency in English by this time was very good, though marked with an obvious accent.

When Edward Koletzkij died at age sixty-five, he left his entire fortune to Katerina, including the large home. Some relatives were incensed with the will, but the Judge had no children, and the will was quite clear. There was no probate and no contest.

The first thing Katerina did was request that Josephine come live with her. By now Josephine was sixteen years old, a very attractive young lady like her mother, and sought after by young suitors. Katerina was very protective of her daughter, strict when necessary, but open minded enough to realize that infatuation, if not love, was an ever-occurring event.

As a result of her inheritance, Katerina now had considerable holdings of real estate within the community. In fact, she was well versed on many of the real estate investments prior to Edward's death. She took an active interest in the various holdings on hand, and in so doing it was necessary to seek advice, so she became a frequent visitor of one of the town's banks.

Within a short period of time, she had sold some land and reinvested in other properties, and each time she closed a business deal, she did so at the bank. Within a few years, she had accumulated even more land and was considered one of the wealthiest women in the community.

She seemed to make very good choices on which land to invest in or which properties to pick up. Her knowledge of the stock market was very good, since she constantly seemed to accumulate wealth no matter what she dabbled in. Both of her sons, John and Joseph had taken wives, and both had farms three times the size of any of their neighbors.

Josephine was the last to marry. She fell in love with a young man by the name of Ernest Pavel. It was not surprising to most, since Ernest was the son of Eugene Pavel, the banker with whom Katerina had had many business dealings.

Some thought there should have been a wedding announcement between Katerina and Eugene Pavel, a divorcee for many years. It was well known that Katerina and Eugene, a highly respected member of the community, had more in common than a simple business relationship. Eugene Pavel had on more than one occasion asked Katerina to marry him. No one understood why, but she refused him each time, and that is why Eugene eventually broke off his relationship with her and married another widowed woman of society.

Over the following years, Katerina became a grandmother several times over, but continued to make considerable investments. She often made trips to Vermillion, Sioux Falls and Sioux City, where she had interests in various banks and in the stockyards. It was rumored, and not without cause, that no matter where Katerina traveled, she had a strong liaison with an influential member of each community.

Some claimed she owned one of the steamer lines between Yankton and Omaha, but if that was the case, she had owned it under another name. Katerina began to travel more frequently, and quite often she traveled with her power of attorney, Raymond Kutilek. Raymond was a widower, but by now her relationships with men, as discreet as they were, more often than not were overlooked by many, since basically Katerina was a good women, and in fact well liked by even the aristocratic ilk.

She became a good friend of the Governor of the Dakota Territory, and was present at the celebration when North and South Dakota were granted statehood in 1889. That was one trip Katerina had made alone. She was gone for three weeks, and when she returned, many wondered, but no one dare ask where she stayed and with whom.

In 1905, she was the first woman in Yankton to own an automobile. She was at that time 65 years of age. The sales representative, who sold her the car, and who supposedly was ten years younger than Katerina, took her on her first drive to introduce her to the automobile. The two did not return for three days. It was rumored that the car had traveled as far as Dante, some 80 or 90 miles away, and that it remained there while certain repairs were made to the broken down machine.

Unknown to the vast majority of the people in the Yankton community, Katerina did not hoard her wealth during her lifetime, but dispersed it anonymously among dozens of charities. She had set up a fund especially for immigrant families who moved to this particular area. When hardships arose, her powers of attorney, and there were many different ones since she outlived most of them, had taken care of the financial donations.

Katerina died on March 4, 1928, at the age of 88. Hundreds of people attended her funeral including her three children, fourteen grandchildren and twenty-six great grandchildren. Of the many people at the funeral, there were those who admired Katerina Dvorak for her benevolence, her courage, and her absolute indifference to the norms of society. Yet, there were just as many present who remembered her mostly as a lady who during her lifetime had had more than an ample amount of suitors. Although the *Stara Kochka* may have been considered a lady with loose morals, there were many women who came to her defense, because she had never once had an affair with a married man.

She had joined a Catholic church in her later years, and some said the only reason she did so was to get enough religion to grant her a place in heaven. Many of the elders of the church knew about her carousing, and after considerable debate, it was agreed that she should not be buried in the cemetery proper. Thus she was buried at the very outskirts.

No one considered that over the decades the cemetery would gain as many inhabitants as it did. Ironically, a visit to the cemetery today would find Katerina's gravestone almost dead center.

* * *

THE HANGING OF FRANK BEHM

The morning broke with a set of dark clouds on the horizon so thick Frank Behm could not see the sun. By six-thirty the sky was still thick with a heavy sense of unforgiving, and it did not appear the day was going to get any brighter. For the last two days it had rained incessantly, but at least for now the rain had stopped. Under any circumstances, the day would not be a bright one for Frank Behm.

Through the bars he could see the townsquare where Charlie Hicks had erected the gallows three days earlier, just before the rain had started. Charlie and Frank had ramrodded cattle up and down the Red together in their earlier years, but those were days when they were young and full of spunk. Charlie never was much of a cowboy. He eventually became a carpenter and Frank went on to become a rancher. It was difficult to say who was the more successful of the two. Charlie barely eked out a living with his trade, and Frank's mediocre size acreage could hardly be called a ranch.

The townsquare was slowly filling up with farmers and ranchers from twenty miles around, most arriving out of curiosity coupled with a shopping trip. There were also those who came for profit— the gamers, the girls from Buckskin Run, the card sharks and some cavalry boys from the army post to the north.

Frank pulled a watch from his pocket. In another thirty minutes or so he would be dead. He had no more put his watch away when he heard the keys rattle in the metal door behind him. It was Sheriff John Krupp, another former cowboy who had turned lawman in his later years.

"How you doin', Frank?" he asked.

"What do you think?" Frank answered.

"Do you want to see the preacher?"

"No, not unless he's got some miracle stashed in his Bible what can get me out of this mess."

"I'm sorry all this happened, Frank. You know I stood up for you best I could."

Frank nodded. It was his own fault. He never denied he had stolen the cattle from Reiker's herd, but it was just to make up for all the calves Reiker's men had branded over the years as maverick cattle—calves that Frank Behm knew were his. That sort of thing had been going on too long, and Frank finally became fed up with it. He could have been a bit more discreet about stealing them, Sheriff Krupp had told him, but Frank was his own man, had his own way of doing things, right or wrong. At the time he had had revenge on his mind rather than common sense, and now he was paying for it.

Sheriff Krupp made a face. "Judge Fuhrman might have been a little more lenient if you just took the cattle, Frank, but you also took a string of Reiker's horses. You know the Judge don't like horse stealing."

"I wasn't stealing his horses," said Frank "There just happened to be a few mixed in with the cattle. I was going to send them back."

"The jury didn't see it that way, Frank."

"Hell, the jury was made up of all Reiker's buddies. Parker, Johnson, Cahill, Ben Fuller and all the rest. Reiker bought 'em off, every one of 'em."

"Casey and Brandt were on your side."

"Yeah, but you can bet Reiker's boys stuck a gun in their face when they was deliberatin'."

"We don't know that for sure."

"I do. Judge Fuhrman knew it too."

"The Judge hanged one of Reiker's men last year for horse

thievin'. I don't think he hardly had much choice but to hang you, too."

Deputy Larry Caldwell came up behind Sheriff Krupp carrying a scattergun, and also had a .45 at his side. Frank didn't even struggle as Sheriff Krupp manacled his hands behind his back. The two paraded Frank Behm out the door and walked him across the muddy ground to where the crowd was gathering.

"Must be three hundred people," said his Deputy. "Gonna be one hell of a send off."

"Shut up, Larry," said Sheriff Krupp.

Judge Fuhrman was waiting for them at the gallows steps, an umbrella tucked conveniently under one arm. Preacher Henry from Buckskin Run was standing next to the Judge, his eyes buried in his Bible, his words of consolation hardly audible to anybody.

The onlookers gathered in closer now, men, women, kids, all anxiously waiting for the event to get underway. Several had parked their buggies at the back of the crowd and were now standing in them as if they were in the balcony of a theater. A half dozen painted ladies lined the steps of the Bone Dry Saloon, all dressed up pretty and ready to return to the dance hall just as soon as the necktie party was over.

Standing near the front were Willie, Justin and Curt, Frank's three hired hands from his ranch. Their horses were tethered to one of the posts holding up the gallows. Alongside their horses was Frank's favorite horse, a red dun by the name of Big Roy.

"Well, boys," Frank said to his cowhands as he headed up the gallows steps, "I see you brought Big Roy for the hanging. Nothing like having the whole family here." None of his boys cracked a smile, but a few in the crowd who heard him and knew the horse seemed to appreciate the comment.

Reiker and his men were off to the side. "Hang the sumbitch and get this over with!" one of them hollered. That got a big laugh from the Reiker hands.

Out of nowhere, a bolt of lightning banged a hellish crash,

which momentarily subdued the crowd. The menacing clouds hung threateningly over the town like some evil shroud as Sheriff Krupp stared up into the black. "Damn poor day for a hanging," he said under his breath.

The rope dangled from a beam above, right over the trap-door. Sheriff Krupp stood Frank in the center of the door, placed the noose over Frank's head and pulled it tight. The crowd was so quiet that one could hear a wagon wheel squeak as a buggy pulled up at the far end of the street.

"Any last words, Frank?" asked the Sheriff.

"Damn right I got some last words." That spurred some laughter from the crowd.

"I want to thank you all for coming to my farewell party," said Frank in a loud voice. A few chuckled with the comment.

"I never knew I had so many friends." More chuckles and laughter.

"When I'm gone, I want you all to go over to the Bone Dry Saloon and have one on me."

Cheers sprang from the crowd along with a light applaud.

"You men out there, buy your kids some candy and be sure to buy your missus some fancy dress material." The women and kids yelled and applauded the suggestion.

"And if you're still here when they bury me, stop by the cemetery on the way out of town and say good bye."

The crowd broke into heavy cheers and yelled their approval.

"I want everybody to have a grand time today, cep'n for you Reiker boys who sent me up here. You boys can go to hell."

The Reiker crowd booed and jeered, but their complaints were drowned out by the cheering and applaud of the crowd.

A light mist crept silently upon the town. Those who had umbrellas pressed them into service. Others pulled up their collars and jammed their hats more firmly in place. Kids huddled under their mother's skirts. Some people headed for the cover of the over-hangs along the storefronts, but nobody left.

Sheriff Krupp pulled a black hood from his pocket. "Did you want this, Frank?"

"Hell, no. I want to see my friends right up to the last."

Those that heard the comment cheered some more.

Sheriff Krupp made sure the noose was tight and positioned Frank in the center of the trap door. He checked his watch. It was one minute to nine.

While the Sheriff waited for the minute to pass, the mist thickened into a steady rain. Finally Sheriff Krupp nodded at the men below, and the pins were pulled that released the trap door.

But nothing happened. The trapdoor did not spring open. Sheriff Krupp stared at the door, looked over at Judge Fuhrman who stomped his foot as a hint.

Sheriff Krupp banged his heal on the trapdoor, but it still wouldn't budge. He thought about asking Frank if he would jump up and down a few times, but it did not seem appropriate.

"Frank, step aside a moment, will you?"

Frank moved over giving the Sheriff some room. The Sheriff banged his heal some more on the door as the wet crowd looked on, some laughter now heard over the pelting rain.

"Come on, get this over with!" he heard Reiker holler.

The Sheriff jumped on the door with both feet, and when the door loosed, he plunged through the opening. A feeble attempt to grasp the wooden sides was useless since the rain created a slick surface, and he couldn't' hold on. He fell through to the ground and groaned when he hit.

Several bystanders came to his aide and helped him to his feet.

He made a few steps but the pain was fierce. "Damn, I think I broke my ankle."

A few men helped him up the stairs once again. Charlie Hicks, who had built the structure, was at the trapdoor checking the opening.

"Must have swelled with the rain," he said. He hollered at

some men below to put the pins back in place. Then Charlie removed the noose from Frank's neck and held on to it with both hands as he stepped on to the trapdoor. He commanded the men to pull the pins again, but the door wouldn't spring. Charlie jumped up and came down until finally the door sprang open and he dropped through.

Though he was holding the rope, it slipped from his hands and he plummeted feet first to the ground. Charlie was shaken, but he came up the staircase and repeated the maneuver again, and after having fallen through a second time, he nodded at the Sheriff. "I think it's safe now."

Sheriff Krupp limped over and placed the noose around Frank's neck again "I'm sorry, Frank. We just ain't having a very good day."

The rain was pouring now and the crowd scattered some more, most heading for cover under the overhangs along the boardwalk.

With Frank in position again, the Sheriff nodded and the pins were pulled. This time the trap door dropped about a foot and hung up again.

"Damn," said the Sheriff. He motioned for his Deputy to help. With Frank still standing in place, Larry banged against the door with the butt of his shotgun, but it still wouldn't drop. By now Judge Fuhrman had climbed the stairs and attempted to shield the onslaught of rain with his umbrella as the two lawmen worked to free the door. With no success, the Sheriff politely asked Frank to step up onto the solid planking of the gallows to give them more room, which Frank did. Charlie Hicks once again climbed the stairs to help, as well as a few of the rain soaked onlookers.

"What the hell kind of carpenter are you, Charlie?" the Sheriff scolded.

"Don't blame me. It worked a few minutes ago," retorted Charlie.

A heated argument broke out between the two. The small, remaining crowd pressed in a little closer taking in the exchange of words. Now, three of the Reiker ranch hands climbed the stairs to render their aid, and a few more men tugged on the door from below.

"Why don't you ask him to just jump off the side?" suggested his Deputy.

"Shut up, Larry," said Sheriff Krupp.

"Boys," cautioned the Judge. "We may have to postpone this."

"No!" shouted one of the Reiker hands. "We'll get the sumbitch fixed!

"You watch your tongue!" the Judge shot back. "You ain't the law in this town."

One of the Reiker hands made the mistake of shoving the Judge out of the way, which brought Sheriff Krupp to the rescue. He whipped a gun from his holster and struck the Reiker hand over the head. Down he went over the side of the gallows flat to the ground.

Now, Reiker himself clambered up the stairs with a few more of his men, and right after them came Frank's three ranch hands, Willie, Justin and Curt. In moments several others from the crowd entered the foray. In no time a dozen men broke into a fistfight, yelling and cursing as Sheriff Krupp stared on, unbelieving at the turn of events. He grabbed the shotgun from his Deputy and pulled back the hammers. When he let both barrels blast, the horses tethered to the post below bolted and jerked out the corner post of the gallows. In a few seconds the entire wooden structure folded over on the side, men falling off, some hanging on, others scrambling to get out of the way. When the structure settled, several from the crowd rushed in to rescue those who were trapped underneath, and in the process Frank Behm slipped off the side of the gallows. With one foot hung up in the partially open trapdoor and the noose still around his neck, he dangled in a prone position, the noose choking the life out of him.

"For Chrissake, cut him down!" someone hollered. Someone sliced the rope and a few men untangled Frank from the trapdoor and laid him out on the ground. He gasped and sputtered when the noose was loosened from his neck, his eyes staring upwards into the pounding rain.

"My God, you damned near killed me!"

In short time everyone had been pulled out from underneath the gallows. Men and women soaked to the bone and covered with mud stood by silently as a few men helped Frank to his feet.

Judge Fuhrman, his face covered with mud and his umbrella ripped to shreds, picked his way through the throng and stood before Frank Behm. In a voice loud enough for everyone to hear, he addressed the crowd. "When you try to hang a man three times and still can't hang him, I believe the Almighty is trying to send a message. Frank Behm, I declare you a free man." The Judge stared at the Reiker group. "And by God, there ain't nobody going to contest this judgement! Court's adjourned!"

The drenched crowd broke into a rousing round of cheer as Sheriff Krupp took the manacles off of Frank's hands.

Amid more thunder and lightning, the rain came down in torrents and the wind whipped through the streets as men and women scattered for cover.

Frank Behm remained in the street, the rain pouring down on him and his three ranch hands.

Sheriff Krupp was a few feet away. "Can I buy you boys a drink?"

"Not today," said Frank.

The Sheriff nodded and limped off with his Deputy.

Frank Behm and his three ranch hands climbed on their horses and walked them down the center of the street. As they passed the Bone Dry Saloon, a piano thumped a lively tune, practically drowned out by the shouts and laughter from the drinkers within.

At the end of the block they set their horses into a lope through the deserted street, splashing up water and mud as they rode. The hanging of Frank Behm was over.

* * *

LAME HORSE'S PROPHECY

Amos Akeley sat on the edge of the grass butte twirling a stem of grass between his teeth. Several miles away to the northwest was the high rising Sentinel Butte, a landmark that could be seen for fifty miles in every direction. To the southwest was Bullion Butte, another landmark, and behind him was Tracy Mountain, all towering about 3000 feet above the lower grasslands, or badlands, as they were termed by the early settlers.

This was Amos' famous spot. From here he could see just about everything for miles, in particular, most of the range land he owned. It wasn't a big ranch compared to the rich ranchers surrounding him, but it was his, lock stock and barrel.

With him was his foreman, Len Quick, a lanky but sturdy middle-aged cowboy. In their earlier years, the two had ridden in many a rodeo, Len on wild broncs since he was so tall, and Amos riding bulls because he was short and stocky, just like his father had been, just like his grandfather had been. Both of the cowboys had been thrown enough times so that they knew about broken bones and lasting bruises. Many times they sat on grassy buttes just like this one, talking about the old days, but today their thoughts were far removed from the rodeo circuit.

"Here comes Lame Horse," said Len as he pointed to the Little Missouri River below. Lame Horse, an old Sioux Indian, always wore a stove top hat and black coat, a trademark that made him recognizable from a mile away. His two grandsons sat next to him in the horse drawn wagon, and riding alongside was another Indian on horseback, dressed for the most part in cowboy attire, although he wasn't a cowboy.

"Looks like he brung Henry Yellow Dog along." Said Len.

"He's a good skinner," said Amos. Amos stuck his fingers in his mouth and gave a shrill whistle. Lame Horse waved back and nodded when Amos pointed he should continue to the east.

Amos and Len mounted their horses and rode across the butte to the far side and picked their way down to the grasslands below just in time to meet Lame Horse's wagon.

Lame Horse tugged on his reins and nodded, a smile tucked somewhere among the wrinkles in his face. His speech was slow, deliberate when he spoke, and for an Indian who had never seen the inside of a schoolroom, his English was very good. "More problems?" he asked.

"Yes," said Amos. He pointed ahead along the fence line. "Four steers, shot no more than a few hours ago. Skin 'em up, leave us a couple quarters and you can keep the rest for your family."

The old Indian nodded, squinted in the hard sunlight at the dead steers. "This is good for me, but bad for you." He seemed to be pondering something. "Bandits, I suppose."

"No, Roswell and his boys, I'm sure, but I can't prove it."

"That's who I meant." said the old man. "If these bandits keep shooting your cattle, I will soon be a fat Indian. Of course, I do not wish to grow fat on your cattle."

"I know that," said Amos. "Now and then they cut fences, sometimes they stampede my cattle, sometimes they just shoot a few."

"That is bad." He nodded, seemed to be pondering something again. "I will have a talk with the Great Spirit about this."

He snapped the reins on his horses and moved on.

"What's this spirit stuff?" asked Len after the old Indian was out of earshot.

"Lame Horse has these talks with the upper world, I guess. His people say he comes up with some astounding information from time to time."

"You don't believe for one minute he's got a connection, do you?"

Amos nudged his horse on. "Well, it comes in the form of a dream for these Indians, some sort of vision."

Len grunted. "If you sit on a mountain and starve yourself long enough, in a couple days you can see most anything."

It was three miles back to the ranch house, and dreams and visions were what the two talked about along the way.

About five o'clock, Lame Horse came into the ranch yard with his wagon. He dropped off two hindquarters and left for his small hut on the outskirts of Medora, the back of his wagon packed with fresh beef and hides.

That night, Amos and Len, along with the four ranch hands had huge steaks and boiled potatoes. Their cook even baked a couple pies for the event. It had been a bad day, but a good night, they all agreed.

The spring in this year was unusually dry for the Dakota Badlands. The days passed into weeks, and by the middle of the summer, Sully's Creek, the only source of water for the Double A Ranch, was running low, the lowest any of the ranchers in the surrounding area of Medora had ever seen. Even the Little Missouri, a mainstay for a water supply, could easily be crossed in a dozen places where a trickle replaced the normal thirty foot span of swift moving water.

The Marquis de Mores, the millionaire Frenchman who owned huge sections of land, was complaining about the drought. He had plenty of water and thousands of cattle, so when he complained every rancher around was within their right to voice concerns.

For most of the summer, Amos Akeley did not have much trouble from the Roswell group. Amos had met Grant Roswell in town on a few occasions, and always, the rich entrepreneur asked how things were going on the Double A, and of course, he had a standing offer to buy Amos' land. Each time they met, the offer was increased slightly, but Amos always held out. He was not about to give up this land he spent half is life working for.

It was towards the end of the summer, when one day the bare water flowing through Sully creek practically came to a halt. Amos was more than curious, even worried about the reason why. He and his foreman, Len, saddled up and headed north along the creek. When they reached his own fence line, they cut the wire and crossed into Roswell's land and followed the dry bed for another mile. In a thicket of trees through which the creek flowed, several of Roswell's men were busy hacking down aspens and placing them across the creek cutting off the water flow.

Roswell himself sat in the shade of a tree, overseeing the project.

Amos and Len slowly walked their horses around the dam amid stares from the Roswell crowd. All work came to a halt when Amos approached Grant Roswell. He was a big man, husky, always wore a white shirt with tan, canvas breeches. Though he usually moved about unarmed, today he was wearing a fancy gunbelt with a pearl handled pistol sticking out of the holster. Neither Amos nor Len were carrying six shooters, but they both had Winchesters in their scabbards.

"Hello, Amos. I guess you know you're trespassing on my land. Come over to get a drink of water, did you?"

All of his hands laughed at the sarcastic comment.

"No," said Amos. "I been following the trail of a thieving skunk, which led me right up here."

"Whoa, that's pretty heavy talk from a fellow who ain't got no water."

"Water or no water, the stench is getting thicker." He looked over the men. "I think I found a den of skunks."

One of the Roswell men grabbed Amos and was about to jerk him out of the saddle.

"No!" shouted Roswell. He walked up to Amos' horse and grabbed his bridle. "I knew you'd come investigating sooner or later. This dam is just to remind you the offer for your place is still open.

I'll even buy your cattle and give you two dollars per head over the going price. And that's a fair offer."

Amos face remained unchanged.

"Tell you what," said Roswell. "You just think it over, and in the meanwhile I'll let some of this water through."

Amos eyed the dam, the trees packed in place. Roswell had a storage pond that ran as far back as a half mile.

"I'm just asking you to think about it, that's all."

Amos eyed the dam again, looked back at Roswell, and then through gritted teeth he said, "I'll think about it."

Roswell nodded with a conquering grin on his face. "Boys, remove that top log."

In seconds a few men hacked at the log with axes and water poured over the dam. Amos and Len turned their horses around and slowly walked away from the crowd. Some laughter and a few rude comments trailed behind them, but neither he nor Len looked back.

For the rest of the summer, water flowed through the creek, but it never achieved the height it once had in past years. The summer heat never let up, and if there was any hint of storm clouds on the horizon, it disappeared long before it reached the Medora country. In fact, the drought was wide spread, the heat and dry winds covering not only the Dakota Territory, but Montana and Wyoming, and as far south as Kansas and Nebraska. The newspapers in all major cities reported similar fears, that this could be the worst drought in a hundred years.

Drought meant short, burnt grass, and that meant the cattle would be lean when winter came on. Pickings would be slim on the plains, which would result in more than the average amount of cattle succumbing to the elements. Amos had come through seasons like this one before, and he was optimistic he could overcome another such season. But with the arrival of fall there was no reprieve, the hot days persisted and any possibility of rain seemed remote. The big ranchers could survive such a winter since they had the conglomerates from Great Britain backing them, stock companies with a lot of capital. Amos could survive too, but the drought would not pass him by without taking its toll.

One evening in late September, Lame Horse arrived in his wagon and came to a stop in front of the ranch house where Amos was sitting on a porch swing. Amos went out to greet him, thinking the old medicine man was just passing through, but Lame Horse tied up his horse and stepped down from the seat.

"I think we should talk," he said to Amos in his slow, deliberate speech.

Amos motioned for him to follow him to the porch, and when they were seated, Lame Horse remained quiet for several seconds, his face twisted as if he were formulating his words.

"I've been communicating with the Great Spirit most of the summer," he finally began. He fumbled in his pockets until he found his corn cob pipe. "I think better when I smoke, especially when it concerns the Great Spirit."

Amos nodded and waited patiently for Lame Horse to go on, until he realized the old man did not have any tobacco. Amos quickly went into his house and returned with a pouch of tobacco and his own pipe. He waited patiently while Lame Horse methodically packed his pipe, his callused fingers pressing the tobacco down to the correct firmness. After they both lit up, Lame Horse crossed a leg and sat for the longest time enjoying his smoke.

"I need to think before I speak," he said, "especially when it concerns the Great Spirit." The wrinkles on his face lifted high when he smiled. "Amos, we Indians don't actually have a conversation with the Great Spirit. We just talk to the Spirit and wait for an answer, and if we get one, it usually comes in the form of a dream. I think you white people call it a prophecy."

Amos was taking in what the medicine man had to say, but after a long lull he prodded him. "So, you had a talk with the Great Spirit, and you got an answer?

"Yes. I am one of the lucky ones. I got an answer yesterday about this time." He seemed to be in a daze for a few moments and then went on. "I got this vision. I saw the land filled with fog or a white smoke, I don't know which. This fog covered a large area, from here to the Big Horns and south for many days journey, you know, Oklahoma."

He puffed on the pipe some more. "And then I saw these mountains on the plains. Not big ones, but small ones, you know, like the size of your barn over there. Maybe bigger. And they were brown. I could hear the mountains speak, but it was not a good sound, more like a groan. Something or somebody in distress."

"And that was your... vision?"

"Yes."

"What does it mean?"

He raised a cheek, squirmed in his seat. "That's kind of the problem. You see, I used your name when I spoke to the Great Spirit, so I figured maybe you could help me solve it. It's a real mystery. Usually I can figure these things out myself, but this one is kind of like a nagging wife. You aren't quite sure what they want, so they don't go away."

The old man puffed some more. "You see, if you understand what the nagging wife wants, then she goes away and you finally get some peace. This vision I had is like a nagging wife, and until I understand what it is, I won't get any peace."

Amos sat back, studied the old Indian. He was so serious when he spoke and so confident his vision bore an important message, yet he was troubled, even had a worried look on his face.

He smiled suddenly. "What do you read from my vision?"

The question didn't stun Amos, but he felt a certain apprehension. Lame Horse had a very good reputation among his tribal members for predicting the future, and now this medicine man was asking him for his opinion.

"I have to think about this," said Amos.

"Yes," agreed Lame Horse. "It is wise to contemplate these things."

A week slowly passed by with each day devoted, in part, to

the vision Lame Horse had presented to Amos. He discussed it with Len, his foreman, but not with the other hands on the ranch. Len had some reservations, but he too, like Amos, had spent many years among the Sioux, and he felt the visions of the Indians had some credence.

After all, Lame Horse had had many visions over the years. He once had a dream in which a great white warrior would lose all of his men to the might of many Indian tribes. This was ten years earlier when General Custer and hundreds of his troopers had been killed in the Battle of the Little Big Horn. Lame Horse was old then, and had been in consul with Sitting Bull when the 7th Cavalry struck. A year later he foresaw the death of the young Cheyenne Chief, Crazy Horse, killed at Camp Robinson where the old medicine man had been living at the time.

He also had a dream in which a white man from across the waters would build a city on the Little Missouri. There were many who scoffed at the idiocy of this vision, Indians and whites alike, at least until the Marquis de Mores arrived. In 1883 the Marquis had built a small town named in honor of his wife, Medora, which had become a gathering place for the surrounding ranchers.

Sometime later Amos and Lame Horse met again, and Lame Horse was now sure what the vision meant. He and Amos spent many hours discussing the dream, and based on the credibility of Lame Horse's former prophecies, Amos Akeley did the unthinkable. He sold his ranch and all his cattle to Grant Roswell, his archenemy, for a price that all ranchers in the community considered an immense sum for his six thousand acre range. Amos made only one stipulation, which Grant Roswell agreed to. He could keep all his horses and spend the winter on the ranch place. With that agreement written on paper and a letter of credit in the amount of $29,000.00, Amos was set. He put Len Quick in charge of the ranch buildings and the men. There was very little to do other than take care of the horses and play cards, which the men did for most of the following months.

In the meanwhile, Amos took the stage to Bismarck where he deposited the money in a bank, and then he headed for Texas where he made arrangements to purchase 2500 head of cattle and a string of horses. The entire winter months were spent rounding up what other equipment he needed, including a chuck wagon. He arranged for letters of credit in a number of banks all the way from Fort Worth to Bismarck, and when spring arrived, he had all his Medora ranch hands sent down to Fort Worth, from where he began the cattle drive.

He picked up four more cowboys and a wrangler to run his remuda of horses, and set out in the middle of April, driving his herd up the Western Cattle Trail. By mid May they reached the Kansas border, and a month later they pushed the herd over the Platte near Ogallala.

From there, Amos grabbed a stage and made his way to Medora a month and a half ahead of his herd.

Lame Horse's vision had turned out to be truer than one could imagine. His vision of fog covering the landscape was snow, a blizzard that devastated the land all the way from Canada to North Texas. The winter started with temperatures that dropped to forty degrees below zero and remained there for days at a time. Snowstorm after snowstorm slowly took its toll on the cattle that roamed the sparse range grass.

Hundreds of thousands of cattle had succumbed to the freezing temperatures, the grasslands covered with several feet of snow. Cattle piled up at fences and died, heaped on each other until they formed huge mounds, the small mountains Lame Horse had seen in his vision. No one escaped the devastating loss that this famous blizzard of 1887 reaped upon the land. The Marquis de Mores, the richest of the landowners, was suffering losses in the millions. All the ranchers around him were bankrupt, including Grant Roswell.

It was a terrible sight to return to this land Amos loved so much. He had seen the carcasses of cattle piled in ravines, left by the thousands upon the prairies to rot, and the stench for miles at a time was unbearable.

But this is what Lame Horse had prophesized, and Amos had been a believer in the Indian's prophecy. On his return to Medora,

Amos had no difficulty in purchasing his land back along with an additional two thousand acres. When the herd arrived in the early fall after a drive of more than 1200 miles, the first real semblance of ranching once again returned to the Medora Badlands.

Lame Horse lived on for many more years in what his friends considered a life of leisure. And whenever he needed tobacco or a beef for his family, he knew where he could find a steady supply.

* * *

HATTIE'S LUCK

Hattie Forester stared through the steel bars of the opening and watched as the sun broke the horizon with a brilliant glow. She had seen a few birds in the past few days and knew spring was upon her. This would be the fourth spring she would witness from this window. A few clouds lay lazily on the horizon, and as the sun rose she marveled how the rays broke around them and shadowed the landscape.

As she looked out the window, a horse and buggy clipped by on the dirt road headed the short distance toward the main street of Laramie. She watched the buggy intently as it passed on the far side of the pond, wishing, like she always had, that she were one of the passengers. She had seen this buggy pass hundreds of times before, almost at the same hour each morning. That was Mr. Sutter, the owner of the dry goods store, she had eventually learned. She would know that buggy anywhere, even on those days when she was awake, lying in the flat bunk against the cold walls. It was the peculiar long stride of the Tennessee Walker that she would instantly recognize.

In fact, she had heard so many buggies pass, she could almost always guess which wagon was passing, simply by the gait of the horse or horses, or by the distinct rattle and creaking sounds that a particular rig emitted.

Her sense of recognition wasn't restricted to buggies. She could recognize certain horses, such as the palomino that had recently appeared on the road. She could discern this particular horse by the hollow sound the front right hoof gave. Evidently the horse had a different size shoe on that foot, or else the horse had a natural gait that simply gave off an odd sound as it passed by. By the rider's attire, she guessed he was a cowboy. He always wore a black wide-brimmed hat and a bright red neckerchief, and though the rest of his clothes were different on occasion, he wore spurs with huge rowels and jingle-bobs that dangled below them. The jingle-bobs alone would give away this rider. The appearance of this rider had started about a month ago she remembered, because some time back out of monotony she began keeping track of various rigs and riders. This particular cowboy always came into town on a Saturday evening, and he always rode in alone.

Hattie let out a huge sigh. Prison life was bleak. Watching the traffic pass in and out of Laramie from inside these prison walls had become her pastime. There was not much else to do. She had some chores to perform for the guards and other inmates of the prison, and she was permitted reading material. Everyday she was allowed a half-hour exercise period outside in the morning and afternoon. But the high walls prevented her from experiencing any view of significance. The only clear view she had of the outside was through this narrow window slot to the east. She had not once seen the sun set since she set foot in this god forsaken building of punishment. She looked at the calendar on the wall. That had been three years, one month and two days ago.

Hattie lowered herself from the window, sat on the edge of her bunk and hung her head in her hands. She had cried almost daily for the first year, but then one day she had cried herself out. The days since then, though tearless, had settled into days of despair and desolation.

Today was no different. The routine would be the same. A call for breakfast usually offered nothing more than some bread or hardtack buns, sometimes accompanied with poorly made gravy. Occasionally she and the other women inmates were given a piece of meat, usually quail or chicken left over from the guards' meal the day before. The noon meal was often much the same, if she had a meal at all, and the evening meal was bread with a potato, if potatoes were in season, sometimes coffee, sometimes tea.

What Hattie missed most was fresh vegetables and fruit. With spring coming on, that meant tomatoes and onions and radishes, and, on rare occasions, apples and pears would be appearing on the menus a little more often.

There were four women in the prison besides Hattie, all four restricted to a portion of the southeast wing. The cells were small with solid walls and a steel door in which a small window opened and closed from the outside. Guards periodically opened this window at random, just to check on the inmates.

She knew the other four women by name. Some others had come and gone during her three-year tenure, but those left, including her, were considered the tougher lot of women criminals. Hattie's sentence was ten years for killing her husband. Her only regret was that she had not poisoned him earlier. He had mercilessly beat and abused her during their short three years of marriage. She had been only sixteen when they married. He was twenty-five and a rounder. From the first day he was chasing other women, coming home drunk, or not coming home at all. The only reason she married him was to get away from her family where her father worked her to death, kept her secluded from everyone and anything for sixteen long years. She thought her life might improve when she married Ike, but that was not the case. So to rid herself from the unpardonable life she had cast upon herself, she had put poison in his meals over a period of three weeks. At first the authorities thought he simply drank himself to death, but during the trial it came to light she had purchased rat poison from an apothecary. A jury comprised of many drunken friends of her husband had convicted her on circumstantial evidence.

There were those that sympathized with her, but that did not prevent her from going to prison. All this took place in Cheyenne, fifty miles to the east of Laramie.

She had a few visitors in the first months of her imprisonment, but ever since then no one had come to see her, not even her mother or two brothers. Her father had been run over and killed by a train about two years ago, she had heard. He was supposedly drunk, passed out on the track. For all she knew, the rest of her family probably pulled up stakes and went back to Cincinnati from where her mother originally came.

Hattie had no idea how she could complete seven more years in this prison. Long ago she had abandoned all hope of a retrial.

She heard footsteps outside her cell, and then came the metal clank as her door swung open. "Breakfast," said the guard as he walked on to the other cells.

Hattie was already dressed and walked down to the privy where she could perform her bathroom chores and wash up before the meal. Three of the other women inmates joined her in short time, and by seven o'clock they were seated in the room where they received their meals. The breakfast was the same, hardtack and some gravy.

"Where's Irene?" asked Hattie when she noticed the young lady was not present.

"She hanged herself last night," answered Bertha, who had served more time than any of the girls. Bertha was an extremely thin person, with a face wrinkled beyond her normal years. She was not an attractive woman, and probably never had been even in her better days.

"That son-of-a-bitch'n Meridin done it to her," said Bertha. "He's been screwin' her for the last month. Poor thing. She was so young and pretty. I'm surprised she didn't hang herself earlier."

The four women ate in silence for awhile. Six months ago a young girl named Cassie Bartholow had managed to reach the kitchen somehow, procured a knife and cut her wrists. They all remembered that incident. That sort of thing in prison was commonplace. Men and women died all the time. Those in the upper echelons rarely carried out an investigation over the death of an inmate.

"Only question is, who's Meridin goin' to pick on now?" said

Bertha as she stuffed down her last piece of hardtack.

A week passed, and one afternoon when Hattie was reading in her room, a guard opened her door and told her to follow him. Hattie hesitated, and when the guard barked at her, she nervously accompanied him down the corridor. They passed the kitchen, a station she had not seen in two years, and went through another corridor to a different wing in the prison. Once there, the guard opened a door and motioned for Hattie to enter. Again she hesitated until the guard spoke. "The man's got pneumonia. The warden says do what you can to keep him alive."

She stared at the man on the bunk. He was in a fever, she could tell, and his breathing was heavy. The cell stunk from urine and feces, something she had been accustomed to, but this smell was extremely heavy.

"What's his name?" Hattie asked.

"Robert Parker," said the guard.

"The warden said I can have anything I need to keep him alive?"

"Within reason."

Hattie knew the death rate in this prison left something to be desired. "Why should this man get preferential treatment over the other men?"

"I don't make the damn rules, lady," the guard snapped.

Hattie sprang into action. "I want plenty of hot water and soap," she told the guard. "Bring me a fresh change of clothes for him and clean blankets. I'll need a disinfectant, a pan of cold water and towels. See if you can get me some laudanum."

The guard left immediately. Hattie was surprised he left the door open. But the man on the bunk wasn't going anywhere, and neither was she.

For three days she nursed him almost constantly. She had scrubbed down the room completely to sanitize it, had bathed him daily, swathed him constantly with cool wet towels and forced the laudanum into him. During this time he occasionally opened his eyes, but she did not think he ever recognized her. He coughed incessantly. In between spells she tried to get hot chicken broth down his throat. It all seemed futile, but on the fourth day, the man opened his eyes and stared upwards at her. She knew he was somewhat confused. He licked at his dry lips.

"Water?" she asked. He nodded.

She dabbed a clean rag into cold water, wet his lips and saw a faint smile come over him. Then his eyes slipped shut again. On the fifth day he was responding even better, and Hattie was taking her minimal nursing skills very seriously. This man's sickness had given her purpose, something she had forgotten about for these three long years.

Two more days passed, and one afternoon while she was silently reading next to his bunk, he suddenly spoke. "What's your name?"

She looked up from her book. "Hattie Forester," she responded, happy to see his recovery was making progress.

"You a volunteer?" he asked her.

"Sort of."

"I have a favor of you," he said.

Hattie's curiosity peaked. "What is it?"

"Can you write?" he asked. She nodded.

"I want you to take a note to a friend of mine."

Hattie smiled. "Where does he live?"

"Just deliver it to the hotel in Laramie. He'll get it."

She laughed. "Is that all?"

"That's right. I'll pay you."

Hattie shook her head from side to side. "I'd like to help you out, Mr. Parker, but I'm afraid I couldn't deliver the note for another seven years."

Robert Parker twisted his face and tried to rise up a bit. She propped him up with a pillow, and as she did so he scrutinized her attire.

"You mean you're an inmate?" She nodded.

He chuckled. "What you in for?"

"I poisoned my husband."

"I'll bet the son-of-a-bitch deserved it."

She smiled again. It had been so long since she had a real conversation with a man or anybody for that matter.

"He sure did," she said. "What are you in here for?"

"Cattle rustlin' and horse thievin'."

"Anything else?"

He grinned. "I done some other stuff, but the law ain't caught me on that, yet."

Hattie laughed out loud. She couldn't remember how long it had been since she had such a hearty laugh.

He looked at her for some time. "Your hair is black as the night. It's nice to have such a pretty nurse at my side."

The compliment took her completely by surprise. It was so nice to hear someone tell her she was pretty.

Then, slowly, Robert Parker slipped off to sleep again. She studied this man carefully. He was rather short, had a squared off face, but a kind one, had sandy colored hair and was a bit stocky, but not excessively overweight. She wondered what he did for a living besides cattle rustling and horse thieving. Or was that his profession?

She managed to get some more broth in him that evening, and by dusk she was back in her own cell. She could hardly wait to see him in the morning and selfishly hoped he would take his time in recovering from the pneumonia. These few days she had spent with him were the happiest of all the days in prison.

She was almost giddy as she began undressing herself for bed. She had removed her clothes completely, stood naked in the candlelight, and then slipped her nightgown over her head. It was then she noticed that the small peephole in the steel door was open.

"Good night, Miss Forester," said the guard as he swung the small door shut.

She had seen only his eyes, but she knew it was the guard

named Meridin.

She did not sleep at all. She was sure sometime during the night Meridin would come into her cell and force her into the demands he had made on Irene. She was not sure how she would react if he did enter. Perhaps he was simply checking on her, as guards normally did. When she first came into the prison she weighed 130 pounds. Now she was somewhere near 105, she was sure. She was thin, and not as pretty now as she once was, or so she tried to tell herself. If she were not attractive, perhaps Meridin would leave her alone. But if he left her alone, that meant he would pick one of the other girls.

Morning came none too soon, and once again she was summoned to take care of Mr. Parker. She spent the entire day with him, but no matter how hard she tried to be cheerful, he could tell she was troubled. He asked if something was bothering her, to which she answered she was not feeling well.

"If there's anything I can do to help you," Parker offered, "just ask."

She wondered what Mr. Parker, an inmate of the prison for only the better part of a month, could do for her. What had anyone done for her since her incarceration to make her life in this hellhole better?

That night Meridin entered her room, just as Hattie feared he might. He sat on her bunk for a moment and said how helpful he might be to her in terms of granting favors, if she in return would grant him some favors. She could smell alcohol on his breath. The mere thought of this man touching her made her shudder.

"I don't want any of your favors," she said as she drew up the covers.

He inched toward her a bit and slowly raised up a hand as if to caress the side of her face.

"Don't touch me!" she warned, "Or else!"

"Or else what?" he asked as he once again reached toward her.

Earlier in the evening she had worked a wooden strut off the bottom of her bed and was holding it firmly in her hand under the covers. She was so quick he didn't even see it coming. The wooden club crashed against the side of his head and sent him reeling to the floor. For a moment she thought she had killed him, but then after several seconds he staggered to his feet. Suddenly he lashed out with a swift blow that knocked Hattie from her bed to the floor. The slaps and blows came one after another, so hard that memories of her husband flashed into her mind. The pain in her face almost moved her into unconsciousness, and she wished it had.

He ripped her gown off, flung her on the bunk and had his way with her. When he left, she lay in a heap on the bed, blood flowing from all corners of her face. A numbing and fitful sleep finally overtook her.

***

On the fourth day, Hattie awoke to see the smiling face of Bertha gazing down at her. After a few seconds, Bertha spoke. "You gave us quite a scare."

Hattie turned her head slowly to scan the room. She was in a larger confinement than her cell. The sun's rays beamed through a window with a remarkable brilliance onto two other empty bunks against a wall.

"Where am I?" Hattie asked.

"In the infirmary. You had a severe concussion. How are you feeling?"

Hattie's recollection of the night with Meridin came into her thoughts. She simply turned her head aside on the pillow and remained silent.

Almost instantly the warden came into the room with another person. He motioned for Bertha to leave, and both men pulled up chairs next to Hattie.

"Miss Forester, this is Dr. Benson. He'd like to ask you a few questions. Do you feel like talking?"

Hattie stared up at the doctor, but said nothing.

"We would like to know what happened between you and James Meridin?"

Hattie's thoughts flashed back to that night. "What do you want me to tell you?"

"The truth," answered the Doctor.

"The truth is Irene Mayfield hanged herself."

The doctor looked at the warden. "Who's Irene Mayfield?"

The warden twisted his face. "She was just a whore who shot two men in cold blood. We tried our best to help her adjust to prison life, but I guess she just couldn't take it."

Hattie rolled her eyes. "The truth means nothing in this place."

"Meridin said he was making a routine check and you accosted him with a wooden club. Is that the truth?" asked the Doctor.

"This woman murdered her husband," the warden told the doctor. "You won't get the truth out of her."

"Do you wish to make a statement?" the doctor asked.

Hattie felt the welts on her face, the cracked skin where blood had dripped from her mouth. One eye was so puffed up she could barely see out of it. "Look at my face," she told the doctor. "That's my statement."

"See what I mean?" said the warden as he stood up. "I'll file a report in the morning. "

With that, the two men left the room. In seconds Bertha came back in.

"Get me a mirror," commanded Hattie.

"You don't want a mirror, darlin'," answered Bertha. "Not now." She cringed every time she looked at the torn face. She bent over and kissed Hattie on the forehead, the only healing power she could give her.

Three days later Hattie Forester was returned to her cell. The doctor had not called on her again. Though she had three open cuts on her face that required stitches, she received no help except for the care and support of Bertha and the other three girls in the prison. A few days later for some reason, the four women had gained new privileges and were allowed to congregate for a few more hours during the day in the room where they normally ate. Exercise outside had been extended to a full hour in the morning and afternoon.

In the next few weeks that passed, Hattie's wounds healed up. She was left with three small scars on her face, but they were not ugly scars, and the redness would disappear in time, Bertha told her.

Hattie had inquired about the man, Robert Parker, whether he had recovered from the pneumonia or not. The information sent through the prison system was often slow, but she learned that he had recovered fully, and he said he would be forever grateful to her for the kind attention she had administered to him.

In the days that followed, the guard, Meridin, began showing up more frequently during the night watch. On one evening he dared to open her door and stand in the doorway like some demigod. "You're lucky you didn't talk," he told her. "If you had, you would be out with Irene now, feedin' the worms."

Hattie sat on her bunk, stared back at him with penetrating eyes.

"Maybe next time you'll be a little more accommodating." Meridin grunted. "And there will be a next time." He slowly closed the door and locked it.

Hattie sat for several seconds in the dark, then pulled the covers up tight against her cheek. As hard as she tried she could not hold back the sobs.

The next day at lunch, Hattie told the girls Meridin had visited her cell again, and that she was sure he would attack her again. The girls could do little but console her, since they knew how punishing and cruel prison life could be. There was no justice of any sort for a murderess in prison, and Hattie knew it.

Bertha had served more time than any of the four women, and she had connections within the prison. On one afternoon when the girls were in the exercise yard, Bertha walked alongside Hattie and grabbed her arm as if to console her. At the same time she slipped a note into Hattie's palm.

"When you get back to your cell, read the note," Bertha said. "And then get rid of it. Understand?"

Hattie was taken by surprise, but she nodded as she tucked the note under the sash around her prison gown. Her heart leaped. She could hardly wait for the exercise period to be over, for she dare not read the note here in the open.

Back in her cell, she was very careful to make sure the guard had walked away after he locked the door. She pressed herself against the wall nearest the door, anxiously produced the note and read it.

He will bother you no more, the note read. The initials *R.P.* followed.

Hattie's mind raced. The note was from Robert Parker, the man she had cared for over a month ago. Not once had she seen him since, but she was convinced it was from him. Bertha would attest to that, she was sure. In moments she destroyed the note, like Bertha had informed her.

The rest of the afternoon she could not remotely read anything, although she tried. Instead, she looked out the window at the various buggies and carriages that occasioned by in the distance. Her mind kept coming back to the phrase, *He will bother you no more*.

At six o'clock just short of suppertime, Hattie was sitting on her bunk waiting for a guard to open her door when she happened to hear a familiar sound from outside the prison. She glanced out the window and saw the rider on the palomino. She smiled, happy with herself that she had recognized the horse by the strange sound the right front hoof gave off. While she watched the palomino in the distance, she happened to recollect this was a Thursday evening. The cowboy had never come into town on a Thursday before, always a Saturday night.

And while she was watching the cowboy, he suddenly turned his head in her direction. Hattie swore he was looking at her, but she was at least three hundred feet away. He could not discern her face in the confines of this small window, could he? But he kept looking in the direction of the prison, and she maintained a vigilant watch on him until he disappeared from view.

At supper that night, one of the guards remained in the room during their meal, thus the girls were unable to talk among themselves, at least not about the note Bertha had somehow managed to procure.

That night, while Hattie was reading in her cell, she heard footsteps coming down the corridor. She looked up when she heard the footsteps stop outside her door. Adrenaline pumped fiercely as Hattie stared at the peephole. It opened and a guard looked in briefly, then swung the door shut again. It was not Meridin, Hattie sighed in relief.

In the morning, roll call was a half hour late, and breakfast the same. A guard was in the room with them, but was summoned outside during their meal. The door was ajar, and though the girls all quit eating and had their ears on alert, they heard only bits of conversation, but Meridin's name was mentioned.

For the next few days, Meridin was obviously not on duty. The pipeline through the prison system was a little faster this time, and a day later at an evening meal when a guard was not present, Bertha confirmed it. "They found Meridin three days ago dead in his bed. Word has it he shot himself through the head with his own .44."

The girls were stunned with her words. Bertha went on. "Course, who would believe that. That son-of-a-bitch was too dumb to shoot himself."

The girls burst out laughing, but abruptly stopped when a guard entered the room.

Life in Laramie Prison suddenly became even better. Within a month a new warden appeared, and shortly after that a few of the guards were replaced, and some construction was going on, with many of the male inmates doing a lot of the work. The infirmary was made larger, and inmates were showing up more often for medical attention. Often the cell doors to the girls' rooms were left open, thus allowing the girls to chat with one another for lengthy periods of time in the hallway.

Laundry chores increased for the girls, which they did not mind, since anything to keep them busy was better than the terrible monotony to which they had tried to accustom themselves.

On a few occasions Hattie had managed to catch a glimpse of Robert Parker, and though they were at a great distance from each other, they managed to exchange silent greetings.

Hattie's luck had changed. All the girls' luck had changed.

The fall and winter seemed long, and then one afternoon in early March, Hattie was summoned that she had a visitor. In a room just off the warden's office, Robert Parker met her. This time he was dressed in canvas pants, had on a colorful plaid shirt, and had shiny black boots with spurs on them. He dangled a wide-brimmed black hat in front of him.

"Hello, Miss Forester," he greeted. Hattie could not comprehend what was going on.

"I just got my parole," Robert explained. "And now that I'm a free man I'm allowed to visit anyone here."

Hattie said nothing.

"I just wanted to thank you for taking care of me when I first came to prison. Without your help, I might not have made it. So, I'm very grateful for all you done for me."

"I would have done it for anyone," Hattie responded.

"I'm sure you would have."

A guard entered from the front of the building. "Your escort is here," he told Parker.

The door was wide open, and through it Hattie could see the front gates some fifty feet beyond. On the other side of the gate was a man holding two horses. One of the horses was a golden palomino.

Hattie returned her gaze at Mr. Parker. "And I want to thank you... for your help."

"It was my pleasure," he answered with a smile. "Goodbye for now." He turned, put on his hat and walked across the grounds to the gate, which was opened for him and locked once again. She watched the two riders swing up into their saddles, and in moments they were gone.

She was returned to her cell where she sat for several minutes reviewing the short meeting she had had with Robert Parker. She could not remember the last time she felt this good, and she wondered if she would ever see Mr. Parker again. Five and one half years remained of her sentence. There was a time she never thought she could make it through ten years, but now, maybe she could.

Three months later on a beautiful June morning she was again summoned to the warden's office. She assumed she was going to be given additional duties within the prison, which she of course would have welcomed.

"You've been granted a reprieve by the Governor," the warden said straightforward as he handed a document across the desk. The Governor's signature was there along with the warden's and some other names she did not recognize.

She simply stared at the warden.

He leaned forward. "This is a rather unusual circumstance. From what I understand the Governor made a deal with a certain individual. If you were granted a pardon, this individual promised not to rob any more banks or trains in the state of Wyoming."

Hattie's mouth hung wide open.

The warden handed over an envelope. "This was part of the deal."

She opened the envelope. Inside was one hundred dollars!

"Who's this from?" she asked.

"We weren't given a name by the Governor. But the person who sent it said you would know who it was."

She knew who it was.

"As soon as you gather up your things, you are free to go."

Hattie did not have much to gather, other than the original dress with which she entered the prison. Though she had gained some of her weight back, the dress was still considerably large about the waist, but she didn't mind. Within an hour's time, she said her good-byes to the girls and was once again at the warden's office.

"Someone is here to pick you up," said a guard. He opened the door to the outside, and she stared across at the gate. Beyond it was a buckboard with a man sitting at the reins. Tied on behind was a palomino horse. It didn't surprise her.

She hurried across the grounds, and as she was ushered through the gate, the cowboy dropped down from the buckboard and removed his hat.

She smiled at the young, handsome man. "Where are we going?"

"Butch said to take you anywhere you wanted."

"Butch?" she asked.

"Butch Cassidy, Ma'am. You probably knew him by his given name, Robert Parker."

She had never heard the name Butch Cassidy before. "Are you a bank robber, too?" she asked.

He laughed out loud as he offered a hand to help her up on the seat, but never answered. He turned the buckboard around, and when he reached the road into town, he turned south in the other direction.

She didn't know where they were headed and she didn't care. As the buckboard bounced along, she kept thinking how lucky she was, and not once did she glance back at the prison.

***

To order additional copies of
Charlie's Gold and Other Frontier Tales
please complete the following.

$15.95 each *(plus $3.50 shipping & handling)*

Please send me _____ additional books $ _____ each

Shipping and Handling costs for larger quantites available upon request.

Bill my: ❏ VISA ❏ MasterCard   Expires _____

Card # _____

Signature _____

Daytime Phone Number _____

For credit card orders call 1-888-568-6329

OR SEND THIS ORDER FORM TO:
McCleery & Sons Publishing
PO Box 248
Gwinner, ND 58040-0248

I am enclosing $_____
❏ Check ❏ Money Order

Payable in US funds. No cash accepted.

SHIP TO:

Name_____

Mailing Address _____

City _____

State/Zip _____

Orders by check allow longer delivery time.
Money order and credit card orders will be shipped within 48 hours.
This offer is subject to change without notice.